good deed rain

I Can Only Imagine
Allen Frost

I see your face in every flower
your eyes in stars above
It's just the thought of you
the very thought of you, my love

Ray Noble and his Orchestra
Recorded 1934

I CAN ONLY IMAGINE

INTRODUCTION:

I Can Only Imagine was written on Capitol Hill in Seattle. I lived a block away from The Globe Café and The American Artificial Limb Company. I really had that dishwashing job where my boss would sleep on top of the dryer, hiding, covered in aprons. This was also when I went to the university library and found Kenneth Patchen's books, *See You in the Morning* and *The Memoirs of a Shy Pornographer.* The poetry and agony of those days—or in other words, the stars of this book.

Keep Up Your Spirits was inspired by all those 1940s movies I was watching. Hope and Crosby, Preston Sturges, Irene Dunne, James Stewart, Fred Astaire in *The Sky's the Limit.* Both adventures, *Keep Up Your Spirits* and *The Sun Does Shine,* go hand in hand together, with the lonesome music lovers Owen Little, and the nameless radio DJ.

I set a lot of stories during wartime in America. *White Russia* is another one. (I liked rediscovering Mort Frixon and the flying typewriters.) This was the last book I wrote in Seattle before I left.

I remember writing *Rome Used To Be The World,* in the rented upstairs room in Portland. That was when my friend Mike and I were making our Super-8 movie *Caruso.* My first winter, there was a storm and the Willamette River overflowed into the city. Sylas Warner's movie, *The Ostrich* was actually a project that Mike and I planned to make after our masterpiece. We found our ostrich star working at a 7-11, and the movie was going to be filmed on the run in Safeway. I'm glad Sylas got to create it. I made sure there was an imaginary world where these other realities could happen.

Allen Frost
Friday Harbor, Washington
November 24, 2016

I CAN ONLY IMAGINE

THE WHEELS OF IT HAVE TO KEEP TURNING

THE FIGHT AGAINST THE DRAGON

VOICES OF SPRING WALTZ

THE MAGICAL ABILITY TO BEND SPOONS

PAST THE USUAL STATUES

MY EIGHT HOURS

THESE THINGS HAPPEN ALL THE TIME

THE WATER KEPT GOING ALL DAY

THE VOICE IN THE CENTER OF THE COLD

HAVE YOU HEARD ABOUT THE BETTER WORLD?

ELLIS ISLAND

YOU'RE ABOUT AS MYSTERIOUS AS POSSIBLE

IT'S ALL BECAUSE I'M THINKING OF HER

ALL MY WAITING WAS LEADING TO YOU

ROMEO AND JULIA

JULIA KARENINA

ALL THE WAY BACK TO WHERE SHE WAS

JULIA JONES

IN THE GHOST TOWN OF PLUTO

SUPERMAN UNDER THE TREES

SLOWLY PEELING ONIONS

TURNING INTO WATER

THE MEXICAN VACATION

CONNECTED BY TELEPHONES

THE EYESIGHT OF A LIGHTHOUSE

YEARS BEFORE LINDBERGH

NIGHT OF TROUBLE

BEATLEMANIA AND THE SHOOTING OF
ABRAHAM LINCOLN

INSPIRATION

THE NEW SPIDERS

DOING SOMETHING RIGHT

IT'S ALWAYS A WONDER

SUNDAY MORNING

JULIA'S PLAN UNFOLDED

She can do things to ya
make ya feel peculiya
don't let Julia fool ya
she's a wise girl

Russ Morgan and his Orchestra
1941

THE WHEELS OF IT
HAVE TO KEEP TURNING

My bicycle rattles more and more every day. This city is starting to wear us down. I go over a crashing bump, or fly around a corner too fast and I have to soothe it with words, "Please don't fall apart…Bring me through this day…I need you." Already the front mudguard is held on with twine, and when the back wheel unexpectedly decides to rumba, I'm shaken all around on the seat.

There are all kinds of subtleties involved with this Schwinn, and they are ever changing things. It's interesting; it's like knowing someone you love. Sometimes I write sonnets for this bicycle, in praise of all its characteristics. I wrap them in cloth around the handlebars. I keep writing beautiful things, that way it should never collapse.

It didn't take too long to get where we needed to be, up one last hill and there we were. I coasted around the corner of Deep Freeze Appliance, a brick and cement building cracking and slowly being covered with ivy tendrils, and I steered into the backyard of the place.

A junked forest of refrigerators stood in the weeds and wild flowers, but I know which one Phil lives inside. Anyway, you can hear the sound of his radio from yards away. I stopped and tripped the kickstand.

The metal rattled from the noise blasting inside. I knocked and kept my hand against the refrigerator. Music shook right up my sleeve. I rapped on the door again, knowing he was in there. He just can't hear me with all that racket.

Leaning closer to the white rusting fridge, I

shouted, "Phil!" and suddenly the door flew open, hitting me in the chin, knocking me over onto the ground. I was stunned, the sky lit up with red stars.

"Greetings!" Phil sat up grinning, and he stretched out of his refrigerator like a vampire emerging. The radio became quiet in his hands.

My jaw was numb. When I said hello it felt like I was chewing rope.

"It's Sir Leon Bredpan!" he announced my presence to the yard full of upright and leaning and toppled refrigerators. Then he grabbed my arm and helped me to stand, pulling me out of the dandelion wands, "Knight of the Round Table!"

"That's me..." The setting sun was overwhelming. I backed up against the cold shade of an old fridge.

He laughed and spotted my bicycle. Automatically, he pulled a wrench out of his black leather jacket. "What's the problem?"

"The brakes, the frame, the wheels and spokes...Everything."

"One of these days you should get a new bike," Phil said. He kept telling me I should junk it and let it sit in this field with derelict refrigerators. "This thing's almost beyond repair. There's not a lot I can do." He tightened a few bolts. The spokes bristled out of place in the wheels.

"Just keep it going as long as you can, I don't want to lose it."

"What?" Phil glanced over his shoulder at me.

"You shouldn't go to so many of those loud rock shows," I told him. His hearing would disappear from him by the time he was thirty. He'd be deaf, groping with the mute radio dials impossibly, while I'd still be humming with my Baroque records. "Just do your best, Phil."

"I always do my best."

I had to smile. It's true. He did good work on my three speed bicycle. Phil Ticks, who worked for Deep Freeze Appliance all day and lived in a refrigerator in their back lot, was a mechanical wizard.

"It's hard to find parts for these Schwinn models," he said. "They're ancient history." He tossed his long black hair and stood up and put the wrench back in his pocket. "That should keep it alive for a while longer though." He set it back against the weeds and spindly flowers growing like spiders on the fence. "You bring me some bagels?" he smiled expectantly.

"Of course." I had them in my backpack. I slid it off my shoulder and took them out for him. A year ago, we worked together at Round Table Bagels, that's how I met him. He got fired, but I kept in touch for the sake of my bicycle. The wheels of it have to keep turning.

THE FIGHT
AGAINST THE DRAGON

It's a constant struggle in this America. The sky is weighed down with gray smog and people act like they're under a spell. It's like life in the Dark Ages. Amazing more people don't realize that. And they have the nerve to stare at me as if I'm the one out of time, with my scarlet Round Table Bagel uniform, stitched with epaulets. I'm not out of another century. I'm recognizing this for what it is: the new Dark Ages. There is a shadow upon the land; it has been cast under a spell by industrial sorcery. There are still plenty of dragons too. I've seen them all over the city. I know them in all their forms. They spring before me as I ride my white three-speed Schwinn. I'll be riding downhill past Kentucky Fried Chicken and all of a sudden, a green Toyota is lurching in front of me. Or a giant in Safeway will attack me in Aisle 5. Tonight I was fortunate. Even though it was night when I left the Deep Freeze Appliance yard and looming skyscrapers were blinking like castles, I made it home okay.

The Verona Apartments welcomed me as I descended the hill—tie dye sheets flying in the glowing windows, a jumble of music, stray cats lurking about the spilled garbage, strange characters going in and out of the swinging oak door—it is my shelter. A light rain was peppering the street and I skidded up to the curb and stopped. I picked up the bicycle and staggered through the door, inside the worn carpeted entry. Up the flight of stairs, I live on the third floor, it's a tiring ascent.

The first greeting as I open my apartment

door is the peering heads of my two pleased cats, then as I open the door wider and move inside, there is my poster of Saint George battling the dragon. It's a pullout from a comic book, in clashing red and blue, 3-D if you're wearing the glasses.

VOICES OF SPRING WALTZ

I always pretend. I've never stopped letting my thoughts imagine and let me be in a different world. At an early age I found it necessary to disregard their reality, the reality of the United States of America, because it can be merciless. I have unraveled what is around me and returned it to the Golden Age.

When I get home, I feed the cats purring and twirling around my feet. Oscar and Imogene are their names, named after a famous barnstorming couple from the 1920's. They watched the food can unwind in my hand, brushing me frantically with their tails until I lowered the dishes to them. I put on a Strauss record for their dinner. On top of the speakers I lit white candles, turning my small apartment into a place of waltzing Prussians.

My chair sits by the window. From it I can see the satellites buzzing in the sky. They're brighter than the stars. Listening to the music from that other time in history, I wondered about that sound that returns so beautifully. People don't seem to think and create things like that anymore. They used to dance beside lakes with hanging lanterns... nowadays a shopping mall would be built on that spot, with a parking lot full of sitting, glaring cars and their dull looking slow motion people.

While the cats strolled in from the kitchen to find out where to sleep, I leaned forward and turned on the television. There's a reason I play this electric contraption and it has nothing to do with the shows. I'm not watching a program. I'm watching a channel that doesn't exist. The set lets me peer around the edge of this reality. I have discovered the secret way past the screen.

THE MAGICAL ABILITY
TO BEND SPOONS

I guess I have the kind of mind that is open to these things, like the people who can see UFOs, or the magical ability to bend spoons. In the strangest of places, I have found where I feel I most belong. I discovered the place a long time ago and I keep returning. Why wouldn't I? It's beautiful. Sitting and watching the TV screen, it happens for me. It's supposed to be just static, but the blue screen opens and pulls me inside. I wake up in what I consider to be the real world.

So I have two lives, the one in America where I have to work seven days a week at Round Table Bagels, and this one. The record was scratching along, I was eager to see where I would be tonight.

I'm not sure if it's a trance or what. How can you explain how you fall into a dream, or how you wake up again? Anyway, here's where I appeared…

I stepped off of a boat. It paddled itself backwards from the reedy shoreline, back into the lake, leaving me standing here where the path begins. As I have said, when I am here, it is America that seems like the strange dreamworld, the cruel nightmare. Life is real here.

I'll tell you more about it when you've seen more of what America is like and why I come here. Imagining is what makes me be alive.

PAST THE USUAL STATUES

This is an example of what I'm up against. The buses, newspapers and billboards are plastered with ads for the new Adolph Schicklgruber action-movie, *Damage Control.* Why is America so obsessed with this semi-literate circus strongman? Why does he get fifty million dollars a film? It tells you something about the nature of things in these Dark Ages.

Riding to work in the morning is all downhill. I steer off the main road clouded with traffic and I glide through the park. There is a row of stone heroic statues I like to see in the green: Emily Dickinson, Edgar Allan Poe, Walt Whitman, and there are others too, leading up to the modern ages: Hemingway, Flannery O'Connor and Raymond Carver. Sometimes I stuff little bits of paper, sonnets, into their brick pedestals. They give me the faith I need, pedaling on my way to work, to the restaurant to wash dishes.

At 6:30 it's either blue or gray, depending on the weather. If the sky's really clear, I can see the sun coming up yellow over the water, through the buildings and trees. I must not have been paying attention. Maybe Melville gave me a kick as I passed? The back wheel began to shake hysterically. My bicycle was falling apart again.

Round Table Bagels is only a few blocks from the park, but we were limping, dragging metal by the time we arrived.

MY EIGHT HOURS

I stood next to the blue pilot light and drank my coffee, with towers of pale bagels in dough piles waiting to be cooked. I have to wash the trays, the pots and mixing pans, cups and plates and knives when I finish my coffee. C.C wasn't here yet, there's no rush. For all of his talk about the Navy and duty and Vietnam, his performance here wouldn't win any medals.

Edna always arrived early to open the door for me. Quiet Edna Purviance, the tallest woman I've ever known, is also one of the kindest people in the universe. She sets all the tables in the morning, starts coffee brewing and talks and laughs to me across the room. Before the swarm of customers arrive, before C.C clunks into the parking lot in his G.M and staggers to his bagels, it's really Edna who winds up Round Table Bagels and keeps it running through the day.

It's spring. The front door was open a little. We can hear the rain and the car tires through it and finally the shuffling of C.C.

"Morning," he smiled and took off his porkpie hat. Edna and I waved. She already had a cup of coffee waiting for him on a table.

I supposed I better get back to the water. My eight hours was beginning.

THESE THINGS HAPPEN ALL THE TIME

It was 11:30 and I was surrounded and outnumbered by armies of dishes, knives, and hot pans and C.C was gone from the kitchen. I discovered him by accident when I went to the back room to get another towel.

The top of the dryer was covered with rags and white towels, with C.C's black winter coat at the peak. I took a towel and uncovered him.

Sitting up, he pulled his thick coat back over the warm towels and recurled himself, mumbling.

What can I do about it? He's my boss. These things happen all the time.

Last week, C.C pulled four bags of flour off a tall shelf onto his head. Edna found him that time, ambushed, knocked out cold with flour clouding over him like Hiroshima. We thought he was dead, his eyes stared off into space. Edna called an ambulance and they arrived screaming with blue and red lights. Two men in white suits dragged him out through the dining room on a stretcher while everyone stared in horror.

So I let C.C remain asleep. Edna was rushing back and forth out front. It would be better to struggle on without him. When the lunch crowd was gone, the restaurant would become still, with only one or two people and you could hear the tinny speakers playing 1940's music.

THE WATER KEPT GOING ALL DAY

The water kept going all day until finally after five o'clock I was finished and my body drained around me in the chair.

"You should get a new bicycle," C.C laughed as he sat down with Edna and me. "That thing's in shambles! You get hit by a train this morning?" It was the funniest thing in the world to him. "Maybe you should send it to the Smithsonian," he carried on. "Abe Lincoln probably owned it before you!" C.C imagined himself as a real comedian. He would be royalty in Las Vegas, every night on stage with a fan of kicking dancing girls and thousands laughing at his jokes...It's too bad his talent is being wasted in this job..."Maybe George Washington wrote the Declaration of Independence while riding it!" He laughed until he coughed and Edna and I stirred restlessly.

I smiled for C.C. I thought of him with Dean Martin and I got up and went to make a phone call. I was hoping Phil Ticks could take a look at my bicycle again to see what he could do. I dialed his number and waited hopefully. Once he was in his refrigerator though, he was in another world.

The ringing stopped, "Deep Freeze Appliance. This is Phil."

"Phil, hello, it's Leon."

"Leon! Let me guess," he paused. "Someone stole your bike! We're finally rid of it!"

"No," I said, "I need your help to repair it again. It broke apart this morning. Could I bring it to you?"

"Listen Leon," he said, static crackling, "I

got a good Sears 10-Speed on trade today. Why don't you take it? Please! It's a gift."

He knew I would never do that, so I tightened the screws, "Will you still be there in fifteen minutes?" He was the only one in the city with the Frankenstein ability to return the dead. My bicycle needed him.

"Yeah..." Phil sighed. "I'll be here."

"Thanks Phil, you're a saint." I hung up and gathered up the pieces of bicycle. I would have to carry it all the way up the hill to him on the summit.

THE VOICE IN THE CENTER OF THE COLD

I wondered where he was. I couldn't hear him in the backyard. There was no radio playing and his refrigerator was empty. I placed my bicycle onto the ground and went over to the store's open door. "Phil?" I called. A light was on. It cast long purple shadows towards me in the doorway.

I peered inside. A blue glow radiated from another room around the corner. Pushing the door open, I walked towards the eerie light, past the overstuffed chairs and *Time* magazines. The air was getting colder and colder and I could see my hesitating breath puff in front of my eyes. "Phil?" I said once again before I looked into that refrigerated office. There was no reply but a strange electrical crackling and all that blue. So cautiously I went into the room.

Phil Ticks, wearing goggles, had a stethoscope pressed to a piano sized block of ice. The light was blinking out of it, making blue veins stand out of the gray white. Deeply imbedded in it, I could see a dark shape that Phil was addressing, speaking into a microphone strung by a wire into the block. "Mr. Gortz..." he said nervously it seemed, "You haven't given me a raise in a year and..."

The blue light flickered inside the center of the cold. Shadows leaped all over the walls, across the glass framed pictures of racehorses and James Cagney. Next to the iceberg, dials in a big machine on the table waved needles redly, as Phil listened painfully to the ice with his stethoscope.

All of a sudden, Phil held his hands up, "Slow

down Mr. Gortz, don't get upset!" A little pool of water melted off the corner of the ice. "I know," Phil agreed urgently, "I'm sorry, I know times are tough...Alright, Mr. Gortz," he sighed and picked up the newspaper on his lap. He started reading the Business section, unfolded to the Wall Street stock reports. "Down three and a half...Down nine points..." His finger went down the list, "Down two..."

The dials of the machine on the table spun again in response and Phil nodded to the ice light, saying obediently, "You're right, Mr. Gortz."

Phil listened some more. I could see him mouthing curses at the ice, but then he answered appreciatively, "Thank you. Yes, Mr. Gortz. Sleep well. Over and out." Taking the stethoscope from the ice, Phil crumpled the newspaper angrily. When he stood up and turned around, he saw me. He jabbed his middle finger at the ice. "That guy is an idiot," he said.

"That's your boss?" I asked, though actually I wasn't that surprised; Deep Freeze Appliance was like most companies.

"The guy's such a cheapskate," Phil continued. "He froze himself to save money. And he's still bossing me around." He slapped the block. "Let's get out of here." Phil pulled a light switch and we left the freezing office.

It got warmer and Phil laughed, "So you're finally going to junk that bicycle?" as we walked outside into the sun and weeds covering broken down refrigerators.

"No," I said. "I was hoping that you could repair it again."

"You never give up!" Phil laughed. Out of a

clump of yellow flowers, he grabbed his radio and switched the thing on.

Electric music blasted. Phil always listened to the worst stations, shaking his head and mumbling. I tried to listen through it, towards some sacred center. When you're in the middle of a new Dark Age, the only way out is Renaissance. Isn't it obvious we need to make good things again everywhere?

Fortunately, Phil Ticks is a bicycle craftsman. He is doing his part and still has a good heart like someone from the Great Depression of the 1930's. One of my relatives told me that during that distant time, there were so many poor with no way of getting money, more and more people would trade with talents. Someone would give your house a new window in exchange for a garden. That's what we're doing today: Phil raises my bicycle from the dead and I give him bagels to eat.

HAVE YOU HEARD ABOUT
THE BETTER WORLD?

Back home, I disappeared into the machine like every night. I have to, it's the only place where I feel I'm really living. I've tried out in the world. Every time I venture, it's like the valley of the shadow of death, both my bicycle and I are in danger. I always look for those things that make sense, but like history, it all seems to be behind us. America is in a curse, but not in my world.

The television screen waits to warm up. It's a slow change. After a while a fog illusion swirls across me and I start to see through it and I know I'm back…

We live in a house not far from the ocean. I see the field, the dirt road and she's standing with me. When we stare into each other's eyes we can hear the waves on the shore. We don't have to work in factories or be surrounded by 20th century machines. All the sonnets I've written have been changed into books. That's what I do here. We can spend our time together walking to the beach, exploring, traveling to see friends, talking to each other whenever we want to. We can do anything. It's amazing how different this place is than the other world I live in. When I'm here with her, America is the ghost.

Unfortunately, it always reappeared and took me back. I held her tightly as things began to shimmer. I told her I'll return soon and then we disappeared from each other and I'm in front of the cloudy television.

Cars in the noisy street below, music through the walls, a muffled shouting argument, a knocking on my door. How much time has passed? Sometimes I can be in the other world for what seems like a lifetime and only be gone from America for an hour. There was still someone knocking at the door.

I stood wearily. Coming back always drains me. I wondered who it could be. Not many people know about me. I spend a lot of my time alone.

The cats lifted their heads lazily as I crossed the room to the door and opened it.

A girl from another time was before me. For a couple seconds I was watching Mary Pickford on the screen framed in the doorway. We both just stared. She's got a speech that she's forgotten and I don't really know what to say either. We were breathing so close to each other, then she spoke, "Have you heard about the better world?"

What a thing to ask me! She has read my mind! I'm stunned and overjoyed.

ELLIS ISLAND

Beside her long blue dress she held a suitcase, old and battered and covered with colorful traveling stickers from all over the planet. Like someone on Ellis Island, I invited her in. She was a little shy about something. I hoped she was comforted by the wall pictures of medieval chivalry and my two sleepy cats and the quiet pond-like TV.

"Would you like some coffee or tea?" I asked. "Have a seat, you look tired," though that wasn't true at all; she was covered with rainbows of course. Anyway, she smiled and sat down with the suitcase next to her.

"I'm so glad you asked me about the better world!" I hurried to the kitchen to pour water in the pan. I laughed, "I thought I was the only one who knew."

"Oh no," she called from the other room, "There are a lot of us who know. It always seems like your own discovery though."

I shut my eyes and opened them again, a Buster Keaton way of coping with illusion, but she was still there. I came into the room and sat with her. "How long have you known?"

She pet Imogene, "Well, I've always felt there was a better way." The cat padded up onto her lap. "Then it just appeared to me," she said. "It was so simple, right before my eyes." She smiled so beautifully; anyone who knew had to be happy.

"That's exactly how it happened for me!" I was so excited. The feeling was funny too. We both laughed, experiencing it like another electricity.

I don't know how much longer we talked. I don't even know what we talked about. When she stood up with her suitcase she did say she couldn't stay for coffee—she wanted to, but she had to go, her car was in a tow-away zone. I listened in amazement was she said she wanted to see me again. I know I heard that. I shut the door gently and I began to spin everywhere.

I laughed. I fell in my chair. I couldn't believe that I forgot to ask for her name. I couldn't even remember what color her eyes were, she had stunned me so completely. I should have played music for her, Django Reinhardt, or I could have shown her some sonnets. My head was spinning. Where did she come from? There was a bright singing in the air (I thought it was me, I was nearly dancing back and forth). It came from the kitchen. It was the kettle boiling.

YOU'RE ABOUT AS MYSTERIOUS
AS POSSIBLE

All I could think about was her, walking around with that suitcase, randomly finding me out of all the people in the universe. I stayed up through the night. I forgot all about the TV's world. I didn't want to disappear, I just kept picturing her. I can imagine that knock on the door and her throwing herself around me, "Oh Leon, I couldn't stay away from you a moment longer!" How amazing, it would be, like a song from the 1930's, with the moonlight in the window as we danced to some ancient crackling record.

The cats couldn't sleep either. They watched me for hours, sitting in my chair, staring off at the stars and satellites. Smiling, I was hoping and hoping the night would hurry up and finish because she said she would see me again in the new day. Tomorrow was going to be a long anxious waiting game, splashing through work just to hurry home at five to wait for her.

Thank you for discovering me, I keep thinking. Even though I don't know your name and you're about as mysterious as possible, I can tell you're the one. It seemed like a miracle, like a pyramid levitating off the desert sand...Leon Bredpan has fallen in love with a real girl in this America, someone who is actually interested in him too. Maybe we've been in the better world all this time, just waiting. I can only imagine that a spell has been broken.

IT'S ALL BECAUSE I'M THINKING
OF HER

As I flew through the rain, I pedaled to the beat of a romantic Ella Fitzgerald song in my head. Even the potholes were placed in time, and for once the wet city was responding like a movie set for me. Of course, it was also because she is now somewhere nearby—where I didn't know she was before. The buses crisscrossed my path and the big overhead signs dripped water in pearling streams across me. The air smells sweeter when it's raining, filled with the spilling gray clouds walking in from the sea.

I was smiling, riding through it all and just by luck, I performed a good deed. I was coasting by the Talking Fish Market with its outdoor stands of vegetables and fruit and seafood on ice, when someone asked me where Pike Street was. I pointed the way and waving kept right on pedaling, just like the knight on a widescreen.

Maybe it's all because I'm thinking of her that good things happen in the world around me. Work wasn't even that painful, it hurried along and was over with. All glowing, I told Edna that I was meeting someone after work and she was so happy for me. She asked me her name and I told how I forgot to ask: I always do things out of the ordinary. No wonder I so often don't fit in! I've fallen in love with someone beautiful who thinks like me, with a Portugal sticker on her old suitcase and that's about all I know. Tonight she will tell me the rest and I'm sure it's alright to hope.

ALL MY WAITING WAS LEADING
TO YOU

There are plenty of times when I've waited for a girl who didn't appear. I would show up at a restaurant on time, get coffee in a booth by the window, and then I would wait. The waitress would return a couple of times to refill my cup and I'd be sitting there gothic as the Phantom of the Opera. An hour and a half would pass and I'd finally get up, leave a dollar and a quarter on the table and go. Or sometimes the phone would ring in the kitchen, the cook would answer it and stare out across the dining room. "Hey you!" he'd point his spatula, "Is your name Leon? Phone's for you." I'd stand over there with the prepped vegetables next to my elbow and I'd listen to her apology and I'd have to say that it's alright. I would always be heartbroken. But that was all in the past.

When I got home from work, I took a shower with the bathroom door open so I could hear her in case she knocked or called. I changed into clean clothes and I had an antique record playing over and over again. I wasn't a nervous wreck, but I was getting there. The sky was darker than the night before, when there was finally someone at the door. My heart was beating like Edgar Allan Poe.

"Hello," she smiled, still with her suitcase, just like yesterday, just like a vision and smiling.

I said, "Gee, it's good to see you." Now I saw that her eyes were brown.

"It's good to see you again too," she said with smiles. "I can't stay long though. I had to double park. I just wanted to come by and say hello Leon. And I wanted to ask if you would like to meet me tomorrow?"

"Yes, of course!" I couldn't believe it was going so well. I'd be up all night again, thinking of her and tomorrow too. "I have to work though," I remembered, "I don't get finished until five. But I'll be back here as fast as I can. Is that alright?"

"That would be perfect." She swung the suitcase in her hand. It brushed back and forth against her leg. I also noticed there was a Brazil sticker on it.

Suddenly I asked her, "What's your name?"

"Julia," she said. "Julia Jones."

"Julia Jones," I repeated and her name had already floated into me and settled over everything inside. "I like your suitcase. Julia Jones, the world traveler."

She laughed, "Thank you, Leon."

"How'd you know my name? How do you know me?" Had she always been watching me, somewhere outside my vision? Who was she?

"I tracked you down. I read your name on the plaque outside," she pointed back down the hallway, the way to the stairway leading down. "Apartment 12-D, Leon Bredpan."

I smiled. She was quite a detective. I liked that, very Victorian, foggy moors and London rainy streets. I took the flower out of my jacket, "Here, Julia. You can have this. You can take it with you." I tried not to make it tremble.

Her fingers went around the stem and she touched my fingers too. "Thank you, Leon," she said, with her smooth running words. "Goodbye, Leon. I'll see you soon. Tomorrow."

"Yes. Bye, Julia." I stepped dreamily

backwards into my room, having watched her go
with the suitcase and the flower in her hands.

ROMEO AND JULIA

I kept thinking of places we could go together. The whole city could be shared. I would like to walk through the park with her to see what she thought of all the statues. When I imagined being able to sit with her, holding hands on the bench next to the fountain, I almost rode into a cedar tree. I could see Julia Jones everywhere on the way to work—clouds made her silhouette, she formed in the glass reflections, someone driving a car, and a girl waking up in an apartment.

When I got to Round Table Bagels, put the kickstand down and left the bicycle near the snoring concealed dryer, I must have been daydreamwalking because Edna's laugh startled me.

"You're thinking of her," she put her hand on me. "Did you at least find out her name?"

With a cup of coffee, I sat down and sighed. I had been saying her beautiful name for twelve hours, "Julia Jones. And," I added proudly because it still sounded so incredible, "Julia wants to see me tonight, after work." I dissolved for a moment, then came back. "She's so incredible, Edna," I confessed. "She's like the 19th century and all the music I love. I've never seen anyone like her before, she must have traveled through time. Maybe out of a Shakespeare play, or one of those French court dramas."

"*You* have a girlfriend?" C.C's voice erupted. He stared at me from the kitchen doorway, where he stood with a static dishcloth stuck to his shirt.

"She sounds wonderful," Edna cut in, but it didn't matter what anyone thought. If I had to, I would ride my bicycle up and down the streets all day and night, declaring my love with a megaphone to the city trying to sleep.

JULIA KARENINA

Her car was filled with flowers. When she opened the door for me and I sat inside, it felt like being dropped into the Amazon. I saw parrots flying around, chameleons and singing caterpillars while she walked around to the driver's side. I picked up the book on the dashboard, it was a thick one. *Anna Karenina.* I was so impressed with her I almost kissed her. She reads books, gigantic epic books! Noticing everything, she was getting more amazing all the time.

"Can you hold this while we drive?" she asked and passed me the greatest suitcase on the planet, the one covered with stickers from around the world. "Have you read that book?" she noticed the paperback in my hands.

"No, not yet. I should, shouldn't I?" We were talking about books! "You feel like a century has passed when you finish reading a book like this. After I read *Moby Dick*, I felt like the ancient mariner."

"I know," she agreed, surging us forward into traffic. "I just finished *War and Peace*."

I stared in awe and also clutched the door handle in fear: we were going so fast down the neighborhood streets.

I have to admit she turned out to be the worst driver I've ever known, but I was in love with her, there was nothing I could say. Onto the freeway, we breezed into split second gaps between other cars. She floored it around semis, ran over a cardboard box, and we banked around curves with me pressed to the door and flowers shedding petals all over me.

"Julia Jones," I said romantically, as a kind of prayer I liked to say as often as I could, and she did slow down. Her brown eyes poured onto me. The car slowed into the center lane. "Where are we going, Julia Jones?" I asked like old Hollywood in a tuxedo, even though it was me, wearing a frayed sweater.

"To the airport."

I stared at her mouth as her smile started to laugh. Flowers were falling into her hair and onto her shoulders too. "The airport?" I asked. We're going to run away together, I thought. We're flying to tropical Mexico or the top of Peru.

"We have a mission," she said, determined, as we sped up again. Fast, but her laughing and erratic steering into the exit lane saved the day. She tossed her head and grinned at me and her hand squeezed my hand. Even though it meant that she was driving fifty five with one hand, we embraced our fingers and stared. She has shining eyes. I could feel all the bad years peeling away.

Perfectly timed, she braked the car towards the visitor's parking lot. We spun up the turning ramps at thirty miles per hour. "Remember," she said, "we were talking about our better world? That's our mission here." Her smile.

ALL THE WAY BACK
TO WHERE SHE WAS

She looked like a walking bouquet with all the flowers gathered in her arms and of course we were laughing. I could barely see her through them, also I was laughing so hard there were tears in my eyes. I found her sleeve through all the roses, tulips and marigolds and I led her from the car into the airport. "I've never had a friend like you," I told her as we passed the United Airlines ticket desk with all the people staring. My other arm clung full of lilacs, irises and lilies and a collapsible wooden flower rack. We stopped in front of the blue television monitor showing arriving flights, me and the beautiful swaying hedge-girl.

Julia said, "When's the flight from Los Angeles landing?" She couldn't see, she was blinded by clovers.

I read the blips, "We have an hour."

"We'll have to hurry," she rustled begonias, "Lead the way, Leon."

It was funny going through the metal detector machine, Julia had no steel or iron, just stems and petals. She brushed through and we hurried to the gate. I found a clear space for her to lay them down when we got there. Flowers surrounded her in waves like a Renaissance woman.

"Now..." she bent down and gathered, "We'll have to work fast."

I set up the flower rack, board poked full of holes, unfolding it next to the window with the background of taxiing jets. Let me say that it warmed me, to stand there feeling her so close to me, putting in flowers.

A starchy looking stewardess came up to us. "Excuse me," she trumpeted, "do you have permission to do this?"

"Oh yes," Julia smiled reassuringly (who could resist her brightness). "We're preparing a welcome." Everything was wonderful, the stewardess nodded and walked away. All it took was confidence.

Julia passed me her car keys, "Leon, can you get the rest of the flowers out of the car?"

"Of course," I said. I would reverse gravity for Julia Jones. I'd build another Golden Gate Bridge if she asked me to. I took the keys out of her hand, being sure to touch her palm gently and then I was retracing back to the parking lot, smiling and gliding with the feeling of being in love. I like the airport, the way people rush to each other out of planes. All these travelers from all over America and the world are coming together. It's so simple and so perfect to feel a part of it.

I found her car again, following the soft petal colors of red, yellow, green and blue. Like Hansel and Gretel the dropped flowers led right up to it. There was even her smell inside the car. I was becoming accustomed to her world, it felt exactly right. I could imagine myself with her forever. We could grow old and white haired together and chase around children on Halloween. It was all in front of my eyes.

My arms held the wide bunch of flowers all the way back to where she was setting up the display.

JULIA JONES

I watched the white 767 push towards our gate and slow to a stop and I watched her brown eyes, so eager. She still had not told me who we were waiting for, but we weren't the only ones waiting. There were television cameras set up and flocks of people. The flowers were all displayed, but under a sheet waiting to be unveiled—Julia wanted it all to be just perfect and surprising.

The tunnel doors flipped open. It was almost time. My wonder Julia Jones steadied herself next to the covered flowers. I had already run my forefinger down her arm from her shoulder to her fingers, slowly pretending not to be fallen in love. She held the rope that would unveil all the flowers and watchfully her lovely eyes stared down the tunnel at the passengers.

The cameras ignored the first people off the plane. The tension built, then the air exploded with flashbulbs. A tan blond monster marched out of the tunnel, waving his arms, as everyone chattered and jumped for joy. "It's Adolph Schicklgruber!" I shouted to Julia, but she was turning away, pulling the sheet off the flowers. I looked back. Adolph was kissing a baby, holding him into the lights and laughing, looking around the cameras with his grin. He was wearing an expensive suit and a baseball cap with the name of his new movie *Damage Control* stitched in gold letters. But on the other side of the airport, unnoticed, a miracle was occurring.

I could tell instantly when the flowers were revealed, I could see Adolph's expression change from bright eyed joy into rage. I turned around.

Julia Jones stood next to the display like a game-show nymph in her long dress, smiling. The flowers were beautiful, but they spelled a word. I didn't notice that when I was helping her set it up. Only from a distance did the flowers turn into letters. The airport was silent, no one moved. The baby started crying and Adolph stuffed it back to the mother.

Then Adolph smiled and turned his back. Deciding to ignore our flowers, he poked the baby's arm, "That's quite a boy you've got, ma'am!" He chuckled, "Maybe someday he'll be like me!" Someone took a photo of the moment and that started them all going again. Adolph led them all away from us, talking loudly about how beautiful our city looks from the sky.

"Come on, Leon!"

Two airport security men grabbed the flower stand, wrestled and kicked it down, crunching it up into sticks and pulp. A couple guys with mops and wheeled garbage cans were waiting.

Julia seized my hand and we moved. "For a second there," she laughed as we ran, "I thought he was going to throw that baby at me!" We went down some stairs and slowed to merge with the crowd that stood around casually with their suitcases.

"Julia!" I whispered into her ear. I could still see Adolph's snarl when he saw the flowers. It was the same look he got in *Barbarian Crypt* when battling demon armies. And then it hit me and I couldn't stop laughing, I was bursting, I haven't laughed like that in so long. I couldn't even speak, Julia held my arms. I was choking on the word she had spelled with flowers. She called Adolph

Schicklgruber, *LOSER*.

We staggered with laughing, out the electric airport doors into the parking lot, though another five minutes had to pass before we could drive away.

IN THE GHOST TOWN OF PLUTO

We were celebrating at an all-night restaurant, reading *Anna Karenina* while we waited for our sandwich. Julia was already to Chapter Five, so she filled me in on the plot. I watched her eyes and mouth and her pretty hands. It sounded like the greatest book ever written. Tolstoy was my sudden new hero, I leaned on her and read with her until the sandwich arrived. She quickly flipped the book over into a teepee.

I was going to warn her that I write sonnets and was watching every second for poetry, when two police cars flashed into the parking lot, escorting a limousine to the front doors of the restaurant. In another second, police and bodyguards rushed inside to search for snipers I guess. One of them spoke into a radio and then, regally, Adolph Schicklgruber entered.

"Not again..." I groaned and I slumped down Julia's side. She was laughing, I could feel her ribs (what a thrill!) I couldn't believe it, slowly I looked back. There was a crowd all around him with cameras popping.

"He's following us," Julia observed. She whispered in my ear, "It looks like he's going to give a speech."

Adolph held up his giant hands and smiled, quieting everyone into just snapping cameras.

Julia and I shared our celebration sandwich, staring and waiting.

"Thank you." Adolph beamed into the nearest television camera and acted, "You know whenever I get a break in my busy acting schedule, I come here to Pluto." He rubbed his stomach,

"Their good homecooking takes me back to Bavaria. And it's nutritious too!" Adolph flexed his suit. "Hey! After dinner at Pluto's Family Restaurant tonight, why not go see my new movie, *Damage Control*. Tell them Adolph sent you!" He laughed and looked around, "How was that?"

"That's perfect," someone said, turning off the camera. "That was heartfelt."

"Well..." Adolph clapped his hands, "Let's eat!"

A waitress nervously led Adolph and his retinue to a roped off section in the back of the restaurant. There were even candles on his table, it looked like a scene from *Bronze Age Weapon*, when he was the king of the Vandals. Adolph beheaded about a hundred people in that movie. I took hold of Julia's hand.

I was more affected than her though. She had gone casually back to Tolstoy. Her cheek looked so soft, her eyes were moving down the rows of sentences in the book and her lips smiled a little. This is why I want to be breathing. It was so amazing that she let me be so close, that she wanted me to be. I wanted to thank her, for letting me feel like a person. I was enraptured. "Julia Jones," I said in my most tropical voice, just as the movie star's table erupted with laughter.

We stared, Adolph pointed across the quiet room to us. "Hey!" he called sarcastically, "It's my number one fans!"

Last year Adolph fell out of his usual role to play the hero in *The Ox Bow Incident*. It was a strange change, he wanted a more serious role than his previous film, *Gun Jungle*. He borrowed that Western long silent stare-down, daring Julia Jones in the ghost town of Pluto to challenge him.

Julia put on Southern airs and waved her napkin from the deck of a Mississippi paddlewheeler. "Why it's little ole Mr. Schicklgruber!" she startled, fluttering her eye lashes. "I do declare!"

Adolph glared at Julia. I expected a candlestick to come flying at us, but he backed down. He mumbled something and returned to eating. Things returned to how they were. A reporter pulled Adolph's sleeve and asked him a question about Hollywood. Talking resumed in the room with the clattering of silverware.

SUPERMAN UNDER THE TREES

The dishes were white fish that I kept splashing into an ocean of hot water all morning until my lunch break. As I remembered brave Julia Jones and last night, I felt a need overtaking me. I had to call her. She gave me her work phone number. She works far downtown at a strange place where they make cardboard boxes by the thousands. For my lunch, I'm allowed to leave Round Table Bagels for thirty minutes and I know a phone booth in the park. Only minutes away, I rode my bicycle and she never left my thoughts.

Surrounded by all my favorite statues and trees, I parked and closed the booth door. I felt like Superman. I put a quarter into the telephone, dialed her number and waited.

"Hello," a different woman answered, "Overjoyed Box Makers. May I help you?"

"Yes, is Julia Jones there?" I asked as calmly as possible.

"One moment, sir," the woman told me and switched me to another line.

Beatles muzak tormented my ear—it was almost sad to think that their song could have been tortured into that. I was trapped in the long wait until she answered.

"Hello, this is Julia."

"Oh Julia," my voice collapsed. "It's Leon. How are you?"

For me her voice started to purr, "Leon..." This was when her words started to blur in my ears, musically. I loved to listen to her. Smiling, I looked around at all the statues standing next to the winding path. There were beautiful hundreds of

them listening on the grass, and some were
standing out of the rain, under the trees.

Edna Purviance laughed happily and sat down at my table near the window of cars and people and rainy weather. "You saw Adolph twice in one night!" She thought it was incredibly funny, her long body shook like a tree.

"What's so funny?" C.C asked. He was putting on his coat, paused at the door while we told him.

"What's wrong with Adolph Schicklgruber?!" he interrupted, staring at me when I repeated the airport arrival story. "He's good!" C.C told us honestly, "I'm gonna see that new movie of his...What's it called?" he rubbed his head.

"*Damage Control*," Edna and I smiled together. The city was filled with signs for it.

"Yeah! I'm going to that!" C.C held an invisible machine gun and spoke Germanically, "I'm the Damage Controller."

I burst out laughing, I couldn't help it. I used to be so hidden and quiet, but Julia Jones was waking me up. I tried to stop laughing, but C.C's imitation was still going on.

He was pretending to shoot cars going by on the street. When a police car went slowly past, C.C immediately stopped and fished his coat sleeve on. He pulled his porkpie hat down tight, cleared his throat, quickly saying, "I'll see you folks tomorrow," as he slid out the door.

I was still laughing, Edna had to get up and answer the phone. Often I've wondered what C.C was like in the Navy, during the Vietnam War. Nothing like Adolph Schicklgruber, I'll bet. I imagined him small, oblivious, like a mole holed

up in the galley of a freighter, slowly peeling onions.

"The phone's for you," Edna said and walked back across the room.

Of course, I was hoping it was the wondrous Julia Jones, but it was the complete opposite.

Phil Ticks sounding worried, yelled in my ear, "Leon! You gotta get up here quick! And bring as much ice as you can!"

"What happened?" I asked.

"I can't explain now, hurry up Leon!" Then he hung up. He was in some kind of danger.

"I have to leave, Edna," I waved at her. We keep bags of ice in the freezer. I grabbed a couple and put them into an empty cardboard box.

There were two fire trucks in front of Deep Freeze Appliance. I leaped off the bicycle with the soggy box in my arms and I ran inside. I followed the hose, where it snaked through a dark office room, ending up at a spotlit charred wall with seven firemen and Phil Ticks.

Phil saw me and dropped a handful of wires. "Leon! Quick, bring that ice!" He led me with a flashlight. "There was an electrical fire!" he explained as we ran around the abrupt corner, down the black hall. "Everything's shorted out, I'm trying to repair it."

He pushed open the door to the refrigerated office cave, but the air wasn't as cold as the last time. It was mild—in fact, the ice block was turning into water. A lake was pooling over the linoleum floor. Phil ripped open the ice bags and spread the pieces over his melting boss. "Thanks, Leon. I just hope he stays frozen until I get the electricity working again." He steered the light back to the door and we returned to the firemen.

Phil dove into the wall with pliers and the flashlight. I had to fill out some papers before the crew would take their hose away.

THE MEXICAN VACATION

About half an hour after the fire trucks drove off, Phil got the electricity working again and the boss of Deep Freeze Appliance returned to ice. Phil was relieved, he blasted the music in the tape deck and he promised to buy me dinner.

At seven o'clock, Phil Ticks was paying for a TV dinner for me. He had picked it out. He said it was the best there was. It even had a visionary name...The Mexican Vacation: two enchiladas, beans and rice and a square of cake. Cook for thirty minutes at 375 degrees.

I said thanks. I waved the Safeway bag at him and we left in different directions across the parking lot. I rode my bicycle down the gliding hill back to my apartment with the Mexican Vacation balanced on the handlebars.

"Leon Bredpan," Julia Jones meowed in the telephone receiver, saying my name like no one else ever can. "What are you doing?" her words sly-ed.

"Not much, I just got back from putting out a fire in a refrigerator. There's a Mexican Vacation in my oven." I smiled, "What are you doing?"

"Wow," she marveled and laughed.

When we talk on the phone, it isn't so important what we say, I think it's just to hear each other that we rush to phones all the time we are apart. Her voice is that perfect tone that makes planets go around each other. I carried dollars of quarters in my pockets so Julia Jones and I could talk. I began to notice and map out where all the telephone booths were along my way in the city. I took glowing pride in the sight of all the strings of telephone wires leading me along—the entire city was connected. The seven numbers for Overjoyed Box Makers was rooted in me.

"Do you want to see a movie tonight?" swayed Julia's words and there was barely an instant before my reply.

"Of course!" I said.

She awakened brightly, "Oh, you know what we could see? They're showing a collection of Posie Crutchfield silent comedies."

"Yes!" I agreed electrically. She knew how I felt about the silent age—in the 1920's the best films were made.

"And that's not all," she laughed, continuing, "The actress who played Posie's daughter in *Night of Trouble* will be at the screening tonight."

"I'll meet you there." I hung up in a rush. I was so excited I had forgotten to say goodbye. I had also forgotten to ask where we would meet. I picked up the phone again. On its plastic I pressed Julia's phone number pattern, I can do it without looking, it's a spell shaped hieroglyphic.

THE EYESIGHT OF A LIGHTHOUSE

Before I got to the stairway, I remembered there was still a Mexican Vacation baking in the oven. I couldn't leave it there. It could become The Great Fire of 1993 when someone's cooking burned down half the city. I turned off the stove, waved goodbye to the cats again and ran down the hallway. Outside, I just barely had time to catch the bus in front of Safeway.

The people seated around me on the bus didn't look the way they usually did. That was part of something much larger that I was starting to notice more and more. It could have been just that the winter was ending—it was getting warmer and lighter—but I felt differently in the world, I didn't feel so bound in the Dark Ages. Once you start sinking, there's no end to how dark you can get, it can all become really terrible. Julia Jones showed up just in time, I think. Julia Jones is chipping away at the Ice Age, bringing better weather to chase off the mastodons and saber tooth tigers.

The bus gasped up a hill. I couldn't see much through the steamy black windows, the dots of light the raindrops made. A woman near me was repeating, "twelve bucks, twelve bucks," over and over, counting and recounting on her fingers. I think she is prepared to say it forever like a wobbling perpetual motion machine. But I don't have to listen anymore. My stop was next and I reached to pull the signal wire. "Twelve bucks," she said at the sound of the bell.

We stopped. I stepped off into the light rain and the yellow window bus drove away to the endless tune of twelve bucks.

The movie theater wasn't far down the street, all lit up with neon, and that's where Julia waited, standing under the red awning. It was so nice to see her looking for me, I waved even though I didn't think she could see me.

Julia bent her knees and waved anxiously back. I laughed. She has the eyesight of a lighthouse.

"It's already sold out," Julia seized my arm and pulled me through the door, "but I bought us both tickets. I left my coat over the seats."

The lobby was filled with the shine from bright chandeliers. We squished across the red carpet, showed our tickets and followed a hallway to a gilded door. Inside, the lights were starting to dim. Julia and I got to our seats just as a spotlight hit the gently waving curtained screen.

The most nervous pale man stepped out onto the brief stage and he cleared his throat. "Hello," he said, blinking. "My name is Dean Carping...I'm the curator of the Rare Arts Society. It is indeed a pleasure tonight to be showing the work of the great film pioneer Posie Crutchfield. In 1916, she began her tenure with Cabbage Studios, which resulted in the nine short films we'll be seeing. The last and most famous in the series, *Night of Trouble*, featured Ruth Pingrin as Posie's unruly daughter. This evening, we're fortunate enough to have Ms. Pingrin here with us." He pointed to an old woman in the front row, who creaked an arm in the applause. "And she has consented to answer any questions you may have about Posie or film. Thank you to all of you for your attendance, it's great to see such a turnout and now let's sit back and enjoy our first silent feature, from October 1916 entitled *A Woman's Work*." Dean Carping bowed, stepped out of the spotlight and as the curtains parted across the white screen, he found his seat next to Ruth Pingrin.

Julia Jones squeezed my hand. She loved Posie Crutchfield too. I could barely believe the

way things were changing. And Julia was so happy,
I could watch the film by the emotions on her face,
as Posie disguised herself as a man and flew across
the Atlantic Ocean years before Lindbergh.

NIGHT OF TROUBLE

Night of Trouble ends with Posie's house being spouted into the air when a water pipe bursts underground. With her umbrella in hand, Posie stands precariously in the open doorway. She's smiling down at the rising sun from a hundred feet in the air as the film closes. Applause, the curtains began to slide back over the screen, the lights were returning, then quickly Julia leaned over and kissed my cheek. She smiled and glittered, looked away and started clapping for Dean Carping returning to the narrow stage. He was leading the frail Ruth Pingrin with bird-like care.

Ruth spoke crisply into a microphone that Dean set to her height. "When I was a girl in 1916," she began, "Posie Crutchfield let me be in her picture. I'm almost ninety, but I will always remember that time magically and clearly as the most beautiful dream in my life. I'm pleased that everyone still enjoys her pictures so much, they shouldn't ever be forgotten." She smiled a look at Dean, "I'm ready to answer questions."

A balloonish man in the third row urgently waved his hand and Ruth pointed to him and smiled. "Can you tell us," he asked, "what it was like working with a genius like Posie Crutchfield?"

She nodded, "In those days," she paused, "as in these days too, it was an uplifting thing for a girl to be near such an incredible woman."

"Ms. Pingrin!" someone in the back of the theater shouted down the rows, "How did you feel when she died?"

"Well..." Ruth looked away, "We were all deeply hurt...It was mysterious, America had just entered World War One and Posie disappeared from the steamship taking her to England. To this day, nobody knows what really happened...She's gone though and the world has changed."

A girl dressed up like the Posie film character in long black with an umbrella, stood up and asked, "Were you in any other films?"

"No dear, after the war my family moved to another city and I got a job sewing at a factory."

A jack-in-the-box with a question popped up, "Did Posie do her own stunts?" and sat back down again.

"Yes she did," Ruth replied. "Everything you see on the screen is Posie Crutchfield."

"What do you think Posie would be doing today?" someone behind us yelled.

"I don't know..." answered the old woman, "People like her are a rarity."

Gigantically, from the balcony a man in the shadows bellowed, "Have you seen any movies lately?"

Ruth shook her head, "Something happened to the pictures..."

The man in the balcony continued loudly, "Have you seen *Damage Control?*"

It hit like lightning, suddenly everyone in the theater knew. It was Adolph again. The spotlight weaved across the red curtains, up into his box where he grinned and waved.

Suddenly people were shouting and hurtling over seats, while Julia and I hugged together against the stampede and Ruth Pingrin was lost in the dark on the stage.

BEATLEMANIA AND
THE SHOOTING OF ABRAHAM LINCOLN

"We were lucky to get out of the theater," I told Edna in the morning. "I don't know what happened to Ruth Pingrin. I don't know if she got swept away in that rush of people."

"The newspaper didn't mention her." Edna swatted the front page, the photo of Adolph Schicklgruber in a surprise visit to a local movie theater. "It's all about how Adolph stole the show," she explained painfully.

I groaned and poured some more coffee in my cup, "We see the most incredible films made in 1916 and he asks Ruth Pingrin if she's seen his new movie...All hell breaks loose. Julia wanted to go back inside the inferno to look for Ruth, but I wouldn't let her, I held her back. It was like Beatlemania and the shooting of Abraham Lincoln."

Edna pulled the newspaper up to her eyes again, "All the article says is, 'overanxious theater goers enthusiastically greeted Adolph Schicklgruber.' "

"I bet it's like one of his movies," I imagined quietly, "Ruth Pingrin was trampled to death because of him and he's the evil corporateer trying to hush it up with money and bribes."

Edna continued reading from the article, "Mr. Schicklgruber provided a history lesson too, living proof of how sound made the silent movies obsolete. He told jokes, answered questions, plugged his new action movie *Damage Control*, and he sang a pleasant nursery rhyme, all to the delight of those gathered."

The bell attached to the door rang as C.C

pushed in out of the pouring rain. "Did you see the paper?!" he called, "My boy's on the front page!" He held up his copy of the *Times*, Adolph's face all dotted with rain.

The day began that way and slowly dragged me through the dishwashing machine. Julia called just before my lunch break and said that she had a fantastic plan. She invited me to dinner to tell me about it. I concentrated on that, knowing that we'd be together at six o'clock when I got home. Every slow tick of the clock hour hand took a century. There was something wrong with the floor drain, water backed up and flooded over my shoes and even worse, C.C talked about Adolph all day. At least it kept him awake and off of the dryer.

I promised to write a sonnet in praise of the joy I felt when C.C finally left. The kitchen had become a serene Walden Pond. I'd write something about how the dishes are parked in the soapy water like loons. On the way home I would leave the scrap of paper with Thoreau's statue.

I was brooding with the sonnet, putting the last bowl away when I truly heard Julia call my name and my thoughts of her all day became real.

"Hurray!" I cheered and waved the bowl, it slipped but I caught it.

INSPIRATION

Seeing Julia again gave me the inspiration I needed to finish Thoreau's poem. It was small but it kept on in your memory like a skipping stone. I wrote it out quickly while Julia sat reading Tolstoy across the table from me, drinking her coffee.

"Julia Jones?" I said and she looked up from the book, "What if we walk through the statue park on the way to dinner?"

She nodded and held the pages shut over her hand, "Did you know that's my favorite place in the city?" then she leaned close to me and whispered, "In fact, my plan involves the park."

"I'm surprised we never met there before," I smiled. "I go there every day with sonnets for the statues. I must have written thousands of them."

"Three hundred and twenty seven," she said mathematically. "Look." She put her suitcase on the table and opened it for the first time. From it she took a beautiful square-shaped homemade book. Every page was a bright color and pasted in it were paper scraps. "I did see you and I learned about you from all these," she touched the poems in her book. "I've been collecting them for a long time, until I finally couldn't wait anymore. I had to meet you."

"I thought they just blew away at night, or washed away," I mumbled, entranced.

"No," she held the book tightly, "I carry this everywhere I go. That's what the suitcase is for."

I laughed and stared, my eyes were bigger than ever. "Why didn't you tell me before?" I touched her hand, "Why did you take so long?" I loved her fingers, they were different than mine.

I smiled, "You were waiting for the right time? You were researching me, hmmm?" Then I realized something, I cleared my throat, "You didn't read the Emily Dickinson sonnet did you?" I held my breath and my mouth dropped open by degrees as she slowly smiled.

"It's wonderful."

"Oh no," I clasped my hands melodramatically, "that one could get me in a lot of trouble."

She laughed.

"I'm surprised Emily let you take that poem."

"She might have tried to stop me, but I'm much faster than a statue." She put the sonnet book into the suitcase again.

"You've turned them all into a book," I stared as she snapped the gold latches closed. What a discovery, what a sudden feeling.

"I'm glad they didn't disappear, we have them still."

THE NEW SPIDERS

We drove to the park and we walked across the lawn towards the Thoreau statue. He's beside the duck pond with Jack London. The new spiders were trying out their beginning web-making skills in the spring air. We saw some beautiful ones, long crazy suspension bridges and rainbow tangles. When I folded the sonnet into a small shape, I pressed it in the brick pedestal. Julia and I sat down on a bench and she unfolded the poem. I read it out loud for her and she kissed me for the second time.

What a thing to return to, out of the green wet park into the gray parking lot where a policeman was ticketing the only car. His motorcycle blinked red and blue, the radio squawked and he seemed posed next to the car hood.

"A copper," I said and I squeezed Julia's hand.

We walked to the car, and he looked up, the huge helmet and reflecting sunglasses on his odd shaped head. Of course he had a mustache too.

Julia said hello.

He grunted. He took the ticket from under the windshield wiper and held it towards her. "You're parked in a no parking zone."

"Oh no," Julia said.

He gave Julia the ticket, "You have fifteen days to respond to the Central Terminal Court."

"I have to go to court?"

"The instructions are on the back." Officer Billy Tighis put the ticket book back on his belt, with his gun and club.

"Thank you, have a great day," Julia said

as she opened the door for me. She went around to the other side, sat down behind the wheel and stared at the shivering paper. "One hundred and fourteen dollars…That's insane!" Then she looked at me quickly and urgently, "We're not going to let this get to us, Leon. Please, we can't. It's a parking ticket, it's not worth thinking about. It's not what we care about. We have big plans, this isn't going to stop us."

"You're right," I agreed. "That's how I feel about washing dishes all day. Now I just think they are like lily pads leading me to you. We're together. We have a better world in mind and good things to do."

I became very kind and suave, the entire world must have been in awe, as I leaned over and kissed Julia Jones.

DOING SOMETHING RIGHT

Around the city, metal things started to disappear…A mixing bowl, the exhaust pipe of a police motorcycle, chair legs and silverware. Where were they going? Who was taking them? I can only imagine.

The world is filled with strange mystery. It wasn't raining fish, but while I was at work, Phil Ticks called again.

"You gotta help me!" he pleaded. "Can you ride up here as soon as possible?"

"What happened? Should I bring ice?"

"No, it's worse," he said, then quickly, "I have to go," and he hung up.

"Was that your girlfriend again?" C.C laughed and shook his head as he lowered a row of bagels into the boiling water. "Man, she calls you *all* the time! You got her in a voodoo trance, Leon!" He watched the bagels and shook his head. "I would pay *money* to know your secret."

"I don't know," I said.

"You doing something right, boy!" He guarded the bagels, paddling like turtles. "You doing something right, that's for sure!" The bagels hissing underwater were almost done. "That's for sure," C.C muttered.

I left the kitchen to get the next tub of dirty dishes from the dining room. When it's raining, we get a lot of coffee drinkers and they leave the tub piled with their cups. I decided to take my last break. I took off my plastic Round Table Bagels apron and I sat down next to the window. I ate my one millionth bagel with coffee. This one was a bit overdone. C.C must have fallen asleep while it cooked brown. I dipped it in the coffee and it left an oil slick. I didn't really feel like finishing them.

I watched the street instead. The rain bounced on the stopped traffic, then splashed around the tires when the light turned green. I watched faces sail past in a bus. A man hurried after it with a newspaper over his head.

Julia's plan had me staying up most of the night. I had blisters on my hands and a burn on my arm.

IT'S ALWAYS A WONDER

It's always a wonder, going to see Phil Ticks. You never know what to expect. Though the rain had let up and the bicycle rattled along the damp streets, I knew I was probably heading into another storm.

The front door of Deep Freeze Appliance was locked. No one answered so I walked around back, past the blackberries strangling old appliances. It shook on its hinges, but the back door was locked too. "Phil?" I called through the wood, "Hello? Phil?!"

A slow voice growled behind me, "I'm looking for him too."

I turned around and automatically put my hands up.

A blue man with a shotgun stared dangerously at me, until his head began to nod and turn like a top losing its center and speed. I wondered if I should run, but I didn't have time. He stopped winding down, he pointed the gun back at me. "You can help me find him. I know he's hiding around here somewhere." There were hundreds of fridges and places to disappear. "I'll take this half of the yard," he swung the gun unsteadily, "and you look over there."

I kept my hands up, I walked like a scarecrow, repeating Phil's name hesitantly as I went into the maze. A pigeon flew out of an old metal cooler nest.

"Phil?" I croaked, just as my hand was caught while passing an upright freezer.

"Shhh!" Phil turned me around. "My boss is after me. We gotta get him back on ice!" he seethed. "He's on the rampage."

"Phil," I said, "I don't know about this, I've got too much to live for now. I don't—"

"Hey!" a voice yelled over the refrigerators. "Hey, you find him?!"

Phil leaped out of the freezer, "Tell him I'm in there!" He dug himself fearlessly into the brambles, "Push him inside and slam the door."

"Phil!" I hit the blackberry covered porcelain. "I—"

"You got him?" came the groggy boss, stumbling through the weeds.

I said, "He's in here..." and kicked the freezer.

"He'll be sorry I ever hired him." Phil's boss leaned against the door. I opened it for him and he fell right in.

Instantly, Phil Ticks ripped out of the green sharp leaves and slammed the door shut on his boss.

"Perfect!" Phil cried, "Leon, you were perfect! Thank you, you saved me again. I'll never forget, I'll remember this," he prodded my chest.

Phil strained the freezer onto a hand truck. We could hear the muffled thumping inside. "Don't worry," Phil held up his hand, "he'll be alright once I get him back in ice." He heaved and rolled it back onto the overgrown path to the office.

I followed at a distance and when I could, I left as soon as possible.

SUNDAY MORNING

When Julia Jones and I woke up, the sky was a thrilling blue. It painted itself without a cloud in sight in the spaces between the green leaves of the tree outside her window. Birds were hopping and singing like angels in it.

Julia Jones is the warmest person in the world. I know. It fills her inside and radiates out all night long and in the morning, with the fresh breeze and sun, she's lovelier than ever. Heavenly, she stretched her arms and legs and her thigh lifted the sonnet book resting on the tangled covers. Part of the time last night we read the book. I breathed in her ear all her favorite ones. Including the Emily Dickinson poem.

Julia yawned and sat up. I kissed her hip where her soft skin rounds over the bone underneath and she rubbed my neck. "Guess what?" she whispered.

"What?" I looked up to her pretty face and I kissed her again. There was no doubt about it.

JULIA'S PLAN UNFOLDED

Julia's plan unfolded beyond my wildest dreams. The park was filled with eager people. All across the sunny lawns, I'd never seen it so crowded. Even the statues looked surprised. I drifted and saw everything in wonder.

A familiar clown walked around with colorful balloons, passing them out. Phil Ticks wasn't too pleased about being turned into a clown, but I had saved his life after all. It was the least he could do. Julia and I had put him in a bright orange suit with a red wig and we painted his face every color. Children danced and followed him around, tugging for more balloons when they lost them to the wind.

Cameras were set up in a half circle on the grass, pointed at a shape draped with a red, white and blue sheet. Julia Jones was close by, answering reporters, smiling and becoming serious again. She saw me and winked as I walked by.

I passed on to the Round Table Bagels table where Edna sat and gave out free cups of ice coffee and lemonade to the line of people. C.C was stacking a pyramid of bagels.

I waved to Dean Carping standing, waiting next to F. Scott Fitzgerald. He waved back and spilled his lemonade.

Laughing children ran around me dragging balloons to the wading pool.

I checked the plastic digital watch on my wrist. Julia and I got two of them from the gumball machine and we had them synchronized so we would know together when it was time. We didn't have to look though. A police siren and the roar of loud engines told us he had arrived.

The crowd surged over to the yellow tape line as Officer Billy Tighis led a black limousine between the trees. Like *Wagon Train*, Billy held his arm up crooked, trying his best to look the part of a cowboy bringing the stagecoach into the fort. He almost succeeded, until he drove into the curb and somersaulted over the handlebars. The big Harley slid and crashed to a stop with him. Everything today was becoming a dream come true.

The door of the limo lurched open and Adolph Schicklgruber stood into the sunlight. He had the same mirrored sunglasses Billy wore—the pair that was trampled over by Adolph's fans.

I hovered back and watched with Julia Jones, my arm around her waist.

"Karma," she said quietly and kissed me.

Prepared for disasters like this, an ambulance crew carried Officer Billy Tighis away. There were probably always casualties in the wake of *Damage Control*. Adolph Schicklgruber got closer to us, signing autographs, shaking hands on the way.

I kissed Julia and went to go hook up the microphone for her. There were speakers set beside Nabokov and Kerouac.

"Ladies and gentlemen..." Julia's voice came clearly across the park air.

Adolph broke through and stood on the podium with her, grinning. He didn't recognize her. She wore a disguise and a long flowing gown and she acted like someone at a steamship christening.

"Ladies and gentlemen," she repeated, "this is a proud moment for us all. I know this man needs no explanation. We've all seen his films. His product is the product of America and we have chosen to honor that proud commitment to excellence with a monument. A testimony to his enduring legacy. Mr. Schicklgruber…" she lifted her arm and pointed to the patriotic sheet rippling in the wind, "This is our gift to you. From all of us, thank you."

Julia passed him the gold braided rope for the unveiling and his giant hands tugged it.

Even my bicycle had gone into the making of the gigantic metal shining head. Adolph gaped, he'd never seen himself look so post-modern, not even in *Robotractor*. The crowd clapped and Adolph began to smile graciously.

He shook Julia's hand and returned to the microphone. "I don't know what to say," he laughed at everyone clapping for him.

Julia made her way to me and put her arms around me lovingly.

A cry ran through the crowd, people were pointing at the big statue and talking excitedly.

Adolph turned around and stared at the sound.

The statue was splitting open slowly like a flower bud. It was a hollow and chambered inside was another red, white and blue sheet. The metal halves of Adolph's likeness fell off to the ground and clanked there on the grass, discarded.

Adolph Schicklgruber cautiously approached the new shape and he carefully unwrapped the sheet.

Such an old woman in black stood there, leaning on an umbrella. At first she looked like she was made of wax, another statue inside of a statue, but then she began to smile. People in the crowd recognized her—she wasn't forgotten any-more, she had returned. Posie Crutchfield looked Adolph straight in the eyes as the people began to cheer and she smiled with wisdom, "We win."

KEEP UP YOUR SPIRITS

Why doesn't the Earth fall?
How can you walk upon it?
It's the music --
It's the music of the Earth
It's the music of the Sun
and the Stars
The music of Yourself
Vibrating

—Sun Ra

stardust, 1945

the first woman in america

sand from guam

lighting up for the night

taxi dancing in a field of stars

paying the fiddler

i'd like to see you

the morning flew out

the beautiful vision

the balloon

you're not alone anymore

in the clouds with a girl

you fell out of the sky

the end of the world

STARDUST, 1945

The sound that played that day was stardust, 1945. Picture the world of that music, when the war was nearly over. There were more and more crazed soldiers drifting back to American shores, where the big band jazz played in waves on every radio and turntable.

While Coleman Hawkins recorded "I'm Through With Love" on February 23, 1945, these two people met like dancers on the floor.

In that winter afternoon, the time must be imagined, they found each other on a famous musical day.

Private Owen Little stepped off the bus and walked through the crowd. He had a blue duffel bag thrown over his shoulder and he staggered under its weight. People bumped into him and spun him in a stream he fought against.

He was practically blind too, his eyes could barely see through his mail-order prescription glasses. "Just like today's movie stars!" the ad in the back of the magazine had promised. While he was stuck on Guam, putting out fires and rebuilding the airfield, he had sent ten dollars to Okinawa for a pair of genuine handcrafted silver-tipped glasses. So he could, "Woo the girls of the USA with handsome eyes!"

On the other side of the street a building blurred. It seemed to hold rooms for rent... Maybe.

A taxi blared in front of him and splashed him with water as it squealed around the corner.

Everyone really is in a hurry in this city, he thought.

An out of focus movie, sped up to clattering dangerous flash.

He waited on the corner step until the line of shiny metal cars with glittering mouths and blasting radios stopped for red.

Struggling to the other side, he threw down his heavy bag. The trumpet inside clanged upon the cement. The windows above the side-walk played dance music onto him. Couples were swinging, changing partners all over the avenue around Owen.

THE FIRST WOMAN IN AMERICA

A long dress swirled next to him, close, the smell of perfume, her enjoying-him laugh. "Welcome home, sailor!"

Owen feebly peered through his glasses. He pushed them down his nose so he could see her… Try. And awestruck, his heartbeat replied.

"You play this gadget?" She held the golden trumpet.

"I," was all he could answer to the first woman in America who had noticed him.

She stuffed it back into his bag for him, among all the snug wrinkled clothes and crushed Pacific shells. "Say…" she smiled, "You should come to The Angel Club tonight." She touched his hand, "If you can play more than taps, bring your bugle, sailor. We need music." Her laugh went into him again and left a red candle burning inside, while she spun and disappeared into the nearsighted water of city crowds.

The glasses worked and Owen blindly, silently, thanked Okinawa.

SAND FROM GUAM

Out of his wallet, sand from Guam poured onto the desk.

The old man with the green visor held his hand open for the payment. The wooden radio played lullabies next to the jar of wilted Canterbury bells.

Owen took some crisp bills, holding them close up to his eyes first to make sure they were enough, before he passed them over.

"Here's your key, Mister Little." The man swiveled behind the counter, to the rack on the wall. "Room twenty two," he said.

Then "room twenty two!" was repeated in a terrible sounding squawk.

Owen looked over his obscuring glasses for a hidden parrot.

"That's right, Milo," the old man chuckled. "This is Mister Little, Milo. He's our new tenant."

"Hello, Milo," Owen waved, still vainly searching the walls and ceiling for a cage or a peg with the annoying bird.

"Down here, four eyes!" cawed a smeary shape on a chair.

Squinting, Owen could make out a tiny bright colored thing. Green feathers, he guessed. "Hello, Milo," he clucked again in a toy voice. "Sorry I don't have a cracker for you, Polly."

"*Cracker!*" the voice shrieked. "I ain't no parrot!"

"That's right," the old man picked Milo up and held him closer to Owen. "I'm a ventriloquist, Mister Little," he explained. "This is my partner in crime, Milo T. Smiley."

"Oh, I see..." Owen accepted the small carved hand and shook. "My mistake."

"I'll say!" Milo squeaked and shot his painted eyes in tragic circles.

Owen grabbed his bag and took the key. "I'm tired. I need a nap."

LIGHTING UP FOR THE NIGHT

The sign outside his window crackled to life at dusk and woke Owen up with huge red letters blasting his eyes with Piltdown...Piltdown...the name of his rented home. He lay there on top of the bed. Every couple of seconds the room would fill with bright color, Piltdown...Piltdown...

Through the walls and creaky ceiling came the sounds of the other apartments: music, restless pacing, a loud argument...

Owen couldn't see that the wallpaper surrounding him was peeling in pale blue strips, or that the floor seemed to have burned scars.

He reached towards the wobbly bedside table and felt for his ten dollar glasses. They steadied the blurs.

A dish crashed on the other side of the wall. Pieces fell with sobbing.

Owen sat up and the bed groaned. He stood, leaving the springs to slowly lift the mattress somewhat flat again, while he walked over to the windowsill.

The air blinked Piltdown in tall letters a couple feet away from the glass. More dross neon shimmered indistinctly up and down the street. Clubs were lighting up for the night.

He watched for a while, though he could tell more by sound what was going on. Shoes clattering, slamming car doors, Gene Krupa pounding, a bottle breaking, voices, laughing; it was going to be a wild evening.

A yellow halo across the street, above everyone, glowed on like an opened eye. By straining through the glasses, Owen could make out the blue dancing letters underneath: The Angel Club.

TAXI DANCING IN A FIELD OF STARS

On the dance floor, Edith twirled all night with lonely servicemen and other down and outers. The music she moved to was spinning records out of wooden speakers. That music was accompanied by Owen Little, The Boomerang and Chops—they were the live musicians that the sign outside promised—the clambering and jumpy improvising that jarred behind the smooth wax big band compositions.

After every song, Edith and the other women would collect money from their partners. Then they would drift to the sides, waiting against the varnished field of stars, wallflowering for someone else to find them.

During a break, Owen leaned over to Chops and said honestly, "This is the best job I've ever had." Better than the war and far better than playing for Maury's Five and Dime before.

"You like it?" Chops laughed and took a fast drink from a paper bag. He coughed hoarsely, "You oughta be good here."

"We like how you play!" Vinnie The Boomerang called and shuffled. "I've never heard such crazy stuff. What is that?"

Owen had been throwing in splashes of Rossini and echoed Baroque against their swing of jazz. "I know it's strange what I do. Whenever I start to play, I forget about what people like on the radio. I remember other things and it comes out the way it wants." He smiled.

"Well, it works!" said Chops. He guided his hook of a left hand back to the piano keys, announcing, "It's swing time, boys!"

On the dance floor, Edith held a crippled officer and she waved like a palm tree.

The next song began with Fats Navarro, and Owen picked up his trumpet again, to join centuries.

PAYING THE FIDDLER

It was late when the music and dancing stopped. The trio and girls slumped in weariness. A record scratched at the end of its groove, as a giant round man ballooned from a door opening out of painted clouds on the wall. Even Owen could see him, and he noticed too how everyone grew tense and drew themselves up alertly.

"A good night," the owner of The Angel Club wheezed and wheeled towards them. He slipped his hand into his coat and removed his thick wallet, counting out money, shuffling it and preening out a bit for each of them. The red jewel on his ring finger hypnotized.

"Mr. Fin," Edith spoke up, standing, creasing down her dress. "This is the new horn player, Owen Fiddle."

"An odd name for a trumpeter," Mr. Fin chuckled.

Owen said, "Well..."

"Nevertheless," Mr. Fin put out his hand cordially, "You are a welcome addition to our ensemble, Mr. Fiddle."

"Thank you." Owen swayed awkwardly. He stared at the white carnation pinned to Mr. Fin's lapel.

Mr. Fin leafed through the green. "For you services..."

Then he snapped his wallet closed, put it back inside tailored cloth. "I'll have all of you here on the morrow, I trust," he said crisply, making an elegant small bow that ended his business with them.

Surprisingly graceful, he glided in reverse
back to his clouded door.

The cold air outside was blue and swirled with flying birds of snowflakes. The lighted Piltdown stood like a holy ship plowing through. Edith pulled Owen in the white fall, across the street and she laughed him to the silver doors of the diner. She already knew, anyone could tell, that he was nearly blind, so she ever kindly led him inside, over to a warm booth. Next to them the steamed glass filled with drifting black and white weather. The place was crowded with late night people like them.

Owen removed his opaque glasses to wipe off the spotted snow and fog. How he wished he could tell her that he longed to see her clear.

Edith rubbed her hands, arms and legs and laughed. She signaled the waitress for coffee, a complex hand language that Owen had seen used to guide cargo freighters unwinding mine fields.

"That Mr. Fin..." Owen said, "He reminds me of someone in the movies." He put his glasses back on to look at the washy angel of Edith.

She nodded and smiled and said, "Sydney Greenstreet."

"Right!" It dawned on Owen, *"Maltese Falcon...Casablanca."*

"His idol," she said.

The waitress came by with two cups of coffee. She took them off her arm, rebalancing plates, muttered, careened on to the next table.

"It's funny," he said, "some people turn into movie characters. I used to think of my life as a movie. For years, I tried to imagine myself that way. I was always hoping a camera was sending me in the right direction."

Looking into him, she asked, "Now what do you imagine?"

"Everything," he said. "I have to imagine everything now." He pointed to his eyes, "They're going, I can't see very well anymore."

She sympathized. She held the warm cup in her hands and let out a little dove-like coo. It flew into the birdhouse of Owen, rested soft.

"But I'm hoping my eyes will come back. They should get better. I know they will heal, I have to let them. There's so much I want to see." He swallowed hot coffee. "Now that I'm back in America..." He pushed at the spoon next to his cup so it reflected the diner and after a pause carefully said, "I'd like to see you especially."

THE MORNING FLEW OUT

The sun had arrived. Orange grew at the point where the street went east, while they were still in the diner talking. Edith was telling Owen about Amelia Earhart who once appeared in her town to give a speech on dreams come true. That was just before the aviator disappeared in 1937. Edith had been at the park to listen to her that day.

"It was the strangest thing," Edith said, "to see someone who would soon vanish away in the open sea."

Owen was spinning from a full night of coffee and this girl. It was the first time he had looked into eyes since the war. He could see her sparkling. He could see that everything about her was in her eyes. He breathed and spoke to them, "While I was in Guam, I heard a story about Amelia Earhart."

"Really?" she leaned closer, "What?"

"There was an airstrip on our island. Planes flew in all the time. A pilot told me something once. He swore it was true." Owen hesitated with the cup of coffee and laughed when she touched him so urgently that it spilled cold on the table.

"What did he tell you?" Edith asked. "She's one of my heroes."

"He was lost," Owen continued. "For some reason his compass went in all directions like a broken clock. The radio was like talking into a sea shell, his call for help wasn't transmitting. And his plane was almost out of gas. Everything had gone wrong. So..." Owen held his spread fingers over their table, "He looked for somewhere to crash."

She was close enough that he could see the

way her eyes shut and fluttered closed, picturing in her mind the movie screen of his words.

"The Pacific is filled with as many little dots of islands and reefs as stars. I remember seeing them from the troopship. Still, the ocean is so big, he was lucky to find one then, when his life was in danger. Even luckier, the island was long enough to land on the sand."

Owen lowered his flying hand wings onto her palm, so it was sky meeting ground softly.

"He landed. The plane was fine. He turned the engine off and opened the canopy. He heard birds, parrots, calling in the trees…those swaying tropical palm trees. And as he listened, he heard something else too. It seemed to be music. Getting out of his plane, he followed the sound through the bushes…It got louder and louder. Someone was playing Glenn Miller…A record player with speakers in the middle of nowhere? He couldn't believe it. He kept going through the jungle until suddenly he reached a place where the sight amazed him."

Edith squeezed his hand, "What?" Happily she guessed, "Glenn Miller's lost orchestra on the wing of Amelia Earhart's plane!"

Owen nodded, "Nearly. There was a big band playing in the shadows of the trees. Japanese and Americans were dancing with island girls, there were banners made out of uniforms. He told me that he wandered in among them and he was welcomed."

"And Amelia Earhart lived there," Edith said knowingly.

"Yes, though not only her. Other people too. People this pilot had known and thought died at sea. Everyone, sailors and soldiers and pilots like him who had lost their way, but had miraculously found the island. They were alive again and they told him he must stay—who needed war when this place was here? He could see people who used to be enemies in the war. Now they were laughing and living alongside each other in green huts."

A truck driver came in the door, yawning a trailing cigarette, rubbing the road out of his eyes. He sat on a stool and quickly fell asleep on his arm.

"As good as it was there," Owen continued, "he told me he wasn't ready to be missing from the world. There were still things he wanted to do. The war would end, it wasn't long, and he wanted to go back to America."

"Did the pilot talk to Amelia Earhart?"

"No, but he borrowed gas from her plane."

"Oh," she sighed.

Owen smiled at her. "He said goodbye to her and everyone and in the morning he flew out. Once he was in the air, his instruments began to work again, the forgetful plane remembered how to fly. He found his map, charted a new path and by the end of the hour, he returned to base."

Instead of falling asleep, Owen Little put his hands to making something, his mind racing with thoughts of her, creating. He took out wire from the mattress frame coils, unstrung and bended, the wood of an armrest and bookcase, putting it all together with the cloth from a shirt, adding sweater soft frays and flowers.

Before her doorway, they had held each other, her hands resting on his hips. Remembering centuries of doing this, Edith told him, "We're so much the same," and he smiled with his hands hinged agreeing, "Like two book covers, with words for each other in between." She squeezed him. He ran his fingers along the back of her arms.

Replaying all this over and over, Owen made his present for her. He hammered the last nail into place. There were silver buttons for wheels and a circle from its animal neck made of bird feathers and poetry words.

He turned on the wooden radio cabinet in the corner and when it warmed, he found Mozart. That was the music he wanted to get inside of the gift, so that whenever she moved it by the string towards her, sand colored clarinets would play.

Who has ever shown you this much love? He laughed at the beautiful vision. The sun gave it yellow paint that glowed. Thank you Edith, he wrote on one of the legs. The war could have got to me. Miracle you…You've saved me. He smiled at the wall, where, through wallpaper, she must be asleep. Angel…

An unglued wallpaper torn corner let him

dream through.

And that was the state of his life in 1945, just as the snow was melting away. He could actually say the words, "I love her, I do."

THE BALLOON

Owen thought he wouldn't need his glasses anymore. He put those thick crystal lenses in his coat pocket and left his room, clutching the present in one hand and the trumpet in the other. The door creaked itself closed behind him and clicked.

Edith may be taking him, his heart and feelings, to before the war, but Owen's eyes still couldn't see like they used to. The hallway swirled and the circling lights sparkled like dimes spinning. He kept close to the wall as he walked almost blindly towards her door. He could see her, he knew.

With his shoe he tapped on the wood, feeling warm and nervous.

Someone opened the door. "Edith?" he peered curiously.

"Owen!" she laughed, "We have to get you glasses." She came closer so he could see her in the watery picture.

"I made this for you," he said, forgetting not to be shy.

In a sigh, she took the shape from him. The radio in her room was playing New Orleans jazz. He quickly put on his mail-order glasses so he could try to see more. She was holding it, wearing green, her eyes were swimming like his.

They were both about to talk when her telephone rang.

Her breath let out, "Oh..." She carried the present with her and Owen, feeling weightless, drifted off like a balloon.

YOU'RE NOT ALONE ANYMORE

All the trees and all the colored signs drained off the water of a warm Spring-like rain. Tires spun through making that hissing wet sound in the streets.

Owen stepped out of the diner picturing Edith still as big as a movie in his mind. He would have walked right into the street with that vision, but someone called his name and a sharp blow caught his leg.

"Hey, Owen!" a voice burst from the side-walk. There was only one hand left on him, and it rested the cane back across the wheelchair's arm-rests. The war had also taken one leg and half the other, but still this man had managed to make it back to America. He drummed in The Angel Club. The shortened body folded up in his blue pilot's uniform rattled the wheelchair. "Are you sleep-walking?" Boomerang asked him with a laugh.

"Hello Boomerang," Owen said. "I guess I'm thinking of something else." The people crowding around made curtains opening to the painted doors of The Angel Club. Owen was just waiting for the world to show her again.

Boomerang sighed, "Oh yes, I know, I remember. You're not alone anymore." His fingers tapped on metal. "Well hurry up then. Let's get across the street."

IN THE CLOUDS
WITH A GIRL

There were things happening that he was completely unaware of. What he dreamed and what was real, was already planned like underground flowers to reveal and surprise him.

Owen and Boomerang didn't notice the sailor stalking the entrance of The Angel Club. There were men in uniform just like him with that same look, all over town, all the time, and Boomerang was watching the ground, and Owen was in love with a dancer in the clouds.

The sailor moved like a shark in the passing crowd. His stare scaled over everyone that went by. He quickly brushed past Owen and Boomerang and seized a Marine. It was in his eyes that he was looking for someone's destruction. People formed a circle briefly during the fight then moved on.

Owen stared at a black and white photo of Edith next to the door. Dressed in a long velvet gown, she radiated. So close to real life, on the stale painted pale yellow wall, her photo was a window to travel into.

"Come on," Boomerang said. "She's not far away." He hit the door with his cane and pushed it open. His chair wheels rolled the same record speed scratching inside.

The floor turned into a lake with the coat of wax, illuminating ceiling lights like stars. The whole dark room glowed with reflections.

Owen sighed. There were only a few people here and he was alone without her. Moving towards the chandelier, just staring at its weak orange flickering, he stopped for a couple lovesick minutes.

Chops had to stir him out of his trance, "Wake up, Owen! We have to start playing. What's the matter? You stewed or something?"

When Duke Ellington stopped blasting out of the speakers, it would be time for their crippled jazz to play.

"He's lost it," Chops explained to Boomerang who had rolled beside them.

Boomerang laughed, "He'll be alright. He'll figure it out. He's in the clouds with a girl."

"Can you wake him up for a few hours?" Chops asked.

"Oh sure." Using the hook of his cane, Boomerang pulled Owen over the floor to the dark back wall.

Owen moved like a zombie spellbound by the patterned stars. When the record ended, Boomerang nudged him and sent him dreamily into playing something Tchaikovsky had written for strings.

It was Edith who broke his trance. He hadn't even seen her appear. He only felt the breeze of music change.

"Owen!" she whispered in his ear. "You've got to get out of here!"

He let the trumpet fall away. "Sweetheart."

"No." She shook her head and her lips sunk. "No. You've got to leave this place."

Her face was swirled with sadness. He put his finger to her wet eyelashes. He was going to cry too. "What's the matter, Edith?"

She seized his shirt and took him from the wooden seat. "Follow me."

He fell out of the rest of the band who continued to bleat to the record. They watched him go while they played.

"Owen," she said, "I can't see you anymore."

He could see her shaped with teardrops, though he suddenly couldn't speak. He was melting too.

"There's someone I didn't tell you about. I didn't think it would stop us. But now..." She shook her head and cried. She grabbed him, "Owen, you fell out of the sky. I didn't think you—" Hugging him, she pushed into him, then she opened a door he hadn't seen, sunk into the black wall, and he fell outside into the alley.

The music from The Angel Club blew all around her. She held the door open only a breath. "Go, Owen! Go far away. We can't ever see each other again. Hurry! If he knows it's you, he'll kill you!"

Her hand struck out and pointed, "Leave

and forget all about me!" Then she pulled the door closed.

The building hummed with the dance music coming from inside.

Owen was left in the cold. It was beginning to snow once again.

THE END OF THE WORLD

He could only see what remained in his mind's sight, the shutting door and his miserable stumbled path. Instincts of the past war years had returned to carry him out of danger. Away from The Angel Club, towards the water on a spinning city colored top. He had slipped to the edge of America where he fell off.

In the darkness of the waterfront, he was able to wind crazily onto a dock, over the hull of a rested shape. He found somewhere to hide in the mess on deck, all heaved with broken shapes. The thing smelled like the end of the world, but Owen collapsed into it and disappeared. In blindness, he only had to wait what seemed a little while for voices and noisy starting engines to toss him to fate.

From the smokestack ahead, sparks would sometimes tear out bright falling meteors against the sky. His mind was swimming. He was just letting the ship take him away. Feeling the throb of engines over water, it didn't matter where it was going, he was through with land. He had been thrown right off.

As he traveled further out to sea, he opened to the black sky. Clouds in the night made gray shapes, edged with moonbeams and in between rang the little stars.

The boat shook through waves. It moved heavily in the winter ocean wind, carrying a huge amount of weight with Owen. The tugboat in front pulled the garbage barge, filled with rotting tons and Owen Little, far out to sea to drop it all into the deep.

THE SUN DOES SHINE

§

At night I hear wings and they bring me words. I wake up when the sky is papery and soft, caught in blue turning dawn color and that's when I write. By the time day is catching on, the sun is showing up with flocks of starlings in the holly tree near my window and cars, more and more, are passing underneath. The words start to fade out stars. I go back to sleep.

I let the Brahms Four Ballads spin slowly disappearing, as Jack Teagarden began to play on the other turntable. For a few seconds, they swam together. The needles throbbed into the red on the console, before I let 1932 come through all the way. The studio of KZRT was filled with crackling record jazz, though sometimes I wonder if anyone outside these walls ever hears.

I was just reading a story, *The Mudlark's Widow*, in the background of Brahms. It's something I wrote this morning. *The rain fell for weeks, changing the ground in a little town.* The pages lay scattered on the floor. I stepped on some, nearly slipped, found a new record and cued it up.

The glass paneled door swung open and Newt Roth the station manager entered. A blue suit, carrying a briefcase, but I knew it was him without turning. His cologne is his calling card. "Evening," he muttered as he quickly passed through to his office on the other side of the room. At this late hour, he comes in to make calls to sponsors, why at midnight I don't know. There are many mysteries here. The next one arrives in fifteen minutes.

§

"The Seattle Fox is in the house!" he announced soulfully as the door vaulted open and he strutted into the studio. Then, *"Man..."* he froze in a captured pose, "What are you playing now?"

"Beethoven," I smiled. We went through this every night, "The Piano Sonata 17."

He was still petrified.

I laughed, "How are you, Fox?"

"Please…" He held up his hand in the most dramatic way while the music continued.

I had to laugh. Last night I left him with a Rossini opera, the night before it was a sound effect record of duck calling. That really threw him. I have a strange sense of humor.

He set up a red heart-shaped candle on the console, impaling it with some incense sticks. "It's gonna take some serious mojo to overcome that sound," he told me with a grin. Digging around in one of his leather pockets, he discovered a matchbook and through his sunglasses he eagerly watched the clock tick towards twelve...A few seconds before, he lit the console assemblage and swung the microphone over to his mouth. He deftly threw the dial, banishing piano from the speakers and suavely began to speak.

"Hello fair ladies, this is your Love DJ, the doctor of sweet sensation, The Seattle Fox." Marvin Gaye crooned in the distance. "I'm waiting for you. Give me a call here at KZRT. It's time to wake up and make love tonight."

It always stunned me the way the switchboard would come to life when he appeared.

115

Suddenly the lights blinked like Manhattan. Once I asked him, "How do you do it? All the lines are lit up."

"Animal magnetism," he explained.

I started to put away my records, half listening to a forlorn girl ask for Fox's advice. A whole city of heartbroken women must have waited for me to get off the air.

"Thanks Fox," the woman sobbed, as he bid her adieu, tipping his fedora to some wilted damsel, then he pressed the next orange button. The incense burned around him, the whole room was clouded with Shalimar.

§

Going home on the bus, I remembered something. I promised to stop by Androcles Perm's Grand Troubadour Exposition. At Cyprus Street, I got out and walked in the rainy shimmer of lights. Androcles' shows usually run past one o'clock, so it wasn't too late to read a story. I had a love story, *She and the Shoefly,* folded up in my pocket.

I hurried on through the misty weather until I reached the door of The Sleepwalker's Café. Guitar reeled outside through a half open window. People stared as I tried to enter quietly as possibly. It was dark enough for me to hide on a broken chair in the corner. Listening to the music, I unfolded the piece of paper and nervously reread my story written there. *She found in the shadow of her shoe, a minstrel fly who begged her to listen to his plea.*

Androcles went into the spotlight while the crowd thanked the guitarist. I let the paper make origami shapes between my fingertips. He introduced me with a flair of his patched jester sleeve and he clapped me on the shoulder, ringing bells. I made it through the cigarette smoke. I don't know why I do this. Maybe I hope in the fablebook promises where just maybe something good will come of it—a Renaissance merchant wants a gold plated billboard made of flowering words for his hanging garden in the mountain tops. It's a surprise for his princess daughter who beautifully sad awaits the wishing well dream of someone to wake her up. I could turn away from this strange lonely life of mine to be in the clouds where every time those wings land on me, someone answers with sighs. I read my story and I thanked Androcles. I waved, then I hurried out the door.

Where the moonlight on a clear night shines on the trees, the birch colored peeling wall of my apartment building appeared. My footsteps echoed on the wet cement pavement. Standing in the yellow floodlit alcove, I finally found my key in a pocket full of pennies, dimes, nickels, string and bits of paper notes. I unlocked the door to a gust of the smell of my home, The Viaduct Apartments. Its old raincoat hallway odor, rushed over stained purple carpets leading to wooden stairs, swept out the door past me like a calico alley cat.

Inside, I climbed the creaky steps. I have a room on the next floor.

A strange kid in a uniform waited beside a door. He held a box of pizza. Music numbed through a wall. He knocked and still waited as I passed.

My door unlocked. I entered, flicking on the light. The walls are papered with my silent movie heroes: Keaton and a girl in a waterwheel, Chaplin holding a flower, Mary Pickford, Harold Lloyd in the rain and a checkered field with Lillian Gish and her sister Dorothy. Roscoe Arbuckle like a black sun on a telephone wire holds Mabel Normand. Marion Davies surrounded by clogs. The record player was still spinning. I forgot and left it turning silently, like a gypsy cart wheel all this time I've been gone.

Throwing my coat over a chair, I needed to rest for a minute.

I could hear my green and white clock ticking. There's rain starting up again on the window pane. It's in a quiet like that that you think about things. I played a record. When it was over I got up and set the needle back at the start again.

Just beginning to fall into the flute and harpsichord, my window started to bang.

I opened my eyes.

It was a shoe tied to string from the room up above. I guess my music is too loud.

Early before the sun, the wings returned again. Right out on my windowsill they landed and told me what to write. I'm beginning to think I have an angel and she has chosen me, flown down miles, picked through a thousand, million faces in America to inspire me. *A Way for the Automobiles*, a story about driving at night, listening to the radio on the way to a drive-in movie. I laughed at the sentences drawn across the gray blue page. The birds in the city were starting to wake, singing tree to tree. Their message to me was to fall back asleep.

When I woke up, evening was sanding all the bright places, white storefronts, sending shadows out to cover over streets bugging with inching traffic. Trees threw blankets on the bucking pavement. I yawned and rolled and with effort sat up on the mattress.

"Good morning," I welcomed the night. I pushed the warm blankets off and stood up. My room was filled with dusky patterns all around the cold walls and floor. Standing in the sirens of arriving dark, I propelled myself to the bathroom and its waiting lion-footed bathtub.

I stood under the hot shower. This evening, it felt I could stand with this water splashing my face forever. Inside one of those drops, I could follow water underneath the ground.

After toweling and dressing, I went to the kitchen and set a silver pan to boil. Continuing the morning ritual, in the other room I started the record player. Waiting for water to be ready, I'll search the tins, drawers and paper boxes for tea leaves or grounds while John Lee Hooker sings.

There are lights of dots in the sky. I wonder if they're satellites or stars or planets I don't know about…something beyond Pluto, shining through our atmosphere. Someone told me you can tell a satellite by staring at it and watching the white dot spin. A satellite is jittering metal shaking in the non-air, while a star stays still as it's always done for years.

Who knows? I know the Milky Way, but I don't know the constellations, the names of stars, or if that's a machine America has trapped up there to broadcast television and send telephone calls across the curve of the planet.

I can't watch the sky for too long. I once loved to, but now I know about infinite. A slip-stream could reach out, catch me, and I may never return.

Here's another laugh for the time I live in now—today I'm dressed as a 1917 Charlie Chaplin. In a soft black vest and hat, I left my room, down stairs, opened the door, and pushing at the warp of the end of the twentieth century, I stepped outside.

I paid a dollar and ten cents to travel on the bus to a street a block away from the radio station.

Looking straight at the black sky, I saw the tall red blinking light at the top of the antenna where KZRT sends out its sound.

Was it always raining? I used my sleeve to dry my face. I felt the soft wet dots on my hand, waiting on the curb for the signal to change.

In KZRT, I waved at the studio window. The DJ before me was playing an old Jack Benny show. I said hello and began to search the tall shelf for Django Reinhardt. I could begin with some of that and then a Mozart clarinet quintet for my new story about automobiles.

§

After I read and got a Carter family record ready to play, the telephone began to ring. That never happened before! It shocked me so much that I nearly dropped John Coltrane. I juggled the flat album and set it down carefully, then picked up the phone, "Hello, KZRT," I said.

"Yeah..." someone squeaked, "Do you know what time it is?"

It took me a second to answer, to read the red digital light on the clock. I said the numbers and whoever it was hung up without another word.

The rest of the night stringed with violins and sitar.

At nearly midnight, The Seattle Fox made his entrance and dramatically fell to his knees in a posture of Mercy Me! "What is it?!" he cried to the heavens, closed eyes hidden behind black sunglasses, tilted head, feather drooped from gray hat band.

I said, "Sidney Bechet."

He struggled out of his deep water trance, "Man, it sounds like something my great grandpa would listen to." Shaking his head woefully, he took my arm, "We *gotta* get you into this century. You've fallen. You're somewhere stuck in the grooves of a hundred years ago."

The Seattle Fox let someone's fluttering heart go as he smiled, hung up the phone and started a crooning love song playing. He stood up and took off the headphones. To rest his voice from all the advising he did and still had to do (the switchboard was filled with sparkling eyes) he danced a little to the music.

I had my coat on. I had a record under my arm and I was ready to leave. I waved to Fox who had spun around to clap his hands in time. "I'll see you tomorrow," I called.

"Hey, wait a minute!" He pointed one of his ringed fingers, "What are you doing tonight? Places to go, people to see?" Slyly he added, "Someone waiting in a window somewhere?"

I laughed, "No. I'm going home to sleep."

Confounded again, Fox stared, even pushed his glasses down his nose to get a clearer look at me. "Going home?! To sleep?! No, no, no. No you're not! It would be sacrilege."

He grabbed me and guided me back to the console, sitting me down in the other chair. A pair of headphones clamped around my ears while Fox commandeered the microphone and spoke.

"From the rainy sky falling, across airwaves into your radio playing softly next to you, this is The Seattle Fox, your Love DJ. How are you, darling? Before I get back to your calls, and I see a lot of you have been waiting—please be patient, ladies—I'd like to see if maybe we can send a friend of mine into somebody's arms tonight."

Oh God! I tore at the headphones and tried to stand, but Fox held me down with one hand.

"You might have heard his show before the Fox arrives...He plays that museum music." The Seattle Fox chuckled at my horrified expression. "I'm just teasing him, folks...Let's hear from the man himself..." He turned to me and pushed the second microphone close, "Tell us what kind of lady you admire."

My mouth was utterly dry. I couldn't speak, until he gave me a shake. "Oh," I said numbly, "Emily Dickinson."

Lights on the switchboard were blinking out fast as fireflies. Fox tried to gain control of the sinking, "No! Like movie stars or something!"

"Lillian Gish," I said. "Mabel Normand... Dorothy Lamour?"

The switchboard had gone dead, a cold black surface.

"Sweet Jesus!" Fox seized the microphone from me. He frantically threw a dial to start spinning a popular record. "You dropped a bomb on me!!" He shook the candle heart at the console trying desperately to resuscitate his show.

While he swarmed over the machinery, cooing into the microphone, waving purple incense clouds and managing slowly to bring a pulse back to the switchboard, I hid around the corner shelf, ducked out of sight. Pretty soon I left.

I felt really sick as I stood at the bus stop. I balanced on the edge of the curb looking down the long stretch of Willow Avenue, wishing the bus would hurry. The Seattle Fox may have had his show derailed, but it was worse for me. I didn't need that. Just leave me in the dark with the records and movies that nobody knows. I groaned.

In that defeated gloom, I was unaware of the person approaching me. Ringing like a trolley, he stopped next to me and piped, "Hello!" It was Androcles Perm with a girl on each arm.

"Oh," I said. My head was swirling.

Androcles wore something made from two different colored suits stitched together. With bells and feathers all over, he looked like two bright circus parrots crushed and joined. He beamed, "How are you doing this marvelous, mystical bewitching eve?"

"Oh," I repeated. "Just waiting for the bus...I have to go home and sleep off a terrible nightmare."

Androcles and the girls laughed. I guess I looked more truly pathetic than Buster Keaton in *One Week*. Androcles put his hand on my shoulder, "It couldn't be so very terrible. Not while Venus shines out there in the stratosphere and sends her servant stars out to make merry lovers of us all." He squeezed the two girls' hips close to his sides.

"I don't know." My downcast eyes caught the reflections of the bus headlights roaring up on me. It finally arrived.

They laughed and waved and carried on in

the night, as I stepped on and lost a dollar fare to a calculator near the bus driver's knee.

§

I was really worried about returning to KZRT. I sat with my breakfast the next night trying to eat it. The coffee was getting cold. I was still fixated on yesterday's disaster. The station manager would probably be waiting for me. In between phone calls, Newt Roth had probably heard my crucified attempt to make contact with the public...What did The Seattle Fox do to me? I was plagued.

I sat watching my oatmeal. My apartment was quiet too. No record player—the shoe had already banged on the window, shutting it down. Whoever lived above me had the ears of a stethoscope.

At last, I pushed the plate and cup away from me. I felt so hollowed out inside, I barely had the strength to leave, but I knew I had to. I closed my door on the black room, walked down the hall and stairs and followed my route to the radio station.

Newt Roth was waiting for me with folded arms. He stood up when he saw me. He paused behind the glass and moved closer as I stepped in. *The Phil Harris, Alice Faye Show* was laughing in the background.

"Step into my office," Newt motioned, turning, chaining me to his cologne wake.

His office was cluttered with stacked papers. There were prizefighters framed on the wall. "Have a seat," he said.

As I sat down, the phone began to ring. "One moment..." Newt picked up the receiver, "Roth here..." He paused and I watched the anger swell red across his face. "Listen, Mitch! Don't threaten me! I should be threatening you! I should send a lead pipe your way is what I should do! Listen to me, I want that money this week... No, this week...Well, borrow it then, I'm sick of waiting."

He hung up suddenly. He breathed deeply and turned his eyes on me. "Now, there's going to be some changes."

I closed my eyes.

I could only see little of the world out the small openings…cars driving past, crowds of teen-agers, a rainbow bunch of balloons, the banner reading KZRT. Then Newt Roth's face cut out the rest of the view. He stood directly in front of me. I could smell him through the costume I wore.

"I'm putting the pail in your hand," he said and I could feel the hoop in my felt paw. "Give everyone a sticker and tell them to listen to KZRT. I'll be back in a couple of hours to pick you up in the van." He slapped my back, "Good luck!" and then he was gone from my restricted sight.

I waddled forward. I couldn't see my feet, I hoped I wouldn't trip. A couple kids walked by so I held out the pail. "Want a sticker?" I asked.

They paused then left, laughing.

"Listen to KZRT!" I called after them.

I kept waddling. Someone I couldn't see hit my felt padded rear end. "Hey Zort!"

I shuffled around and scanned through the eye-holes. Someone behind me pulled my tail and there was laughing all around. I could see people forming a circle surrounding me. Hands I couldn't see ripped the pail from my soft paw. Then I felt the pail shoved down on top of my head. Yellow stickers fluttered past my eyes like autumn leaves.

"Hey Zort!" Two kids from different places behind me knocked me over. It didn't hurt too much, I was padded with inches of green foam, but I couldn't stand up. Then it started to be painful, there were many people kicking me. They really didn't like Zort! I tried to roll away to no avail. Finally I just took my chances and un-snapped the head. I had to get out.

I tossed it up and it allowed me some moments to escape the suit. I squirmed through the hole in the shoulders and left the green skin. It was getting torn apart, I was lucky to get out with only cuts and bruises. The crowd didn't seem to care about me after that. They let me limp away. I sat by a fountain and watched them tear the radio mascot to shreds.

I reached into the shallow fountain water and picked out bus fare. Sometimes a drop of blood spotted onto the pool. I could taste the cut on my lip. This was how that dragon felt after Saint George.

The crowd was done with the forgotten Zort costume. A few late night customers hurried to their parked cars.

I filled my other hand with brown and orange coins, but I only had fifty cents. I kept going around the edge of the pool until I had a dollar. Newt would return to find only pieces of green and no me. I was in no condition to wait around.

Through the parking lot, overhead lamps glowed pink on the wet roofs of cars. I limped past them to the bus stop. What a disastrous night. I couldn't laugh at it yet, I was too hurt, and it was hard to imagine this happening to Chaplin. Both of my scraped hands cupped the cold coins. I stopped and leaned against the bus signpost.

The road was empty. I could see the dot of light in the sky that Androcles told me was Venus. I stared at her softness and with all those wishing-well pennies in my hands, I made a strong prayer.

A few seconds later, an orange tow truck stopped next to me.

Palomino Towing, I read the big letters on the door.

It opened and a girl looked at me.

The driver, an older man, leaned around her to say, "You need a ride?"

I stood there with a hundred pennies staring at them.

"Are you alright?" the girl asked. She moved over to let me in. "Are you hurt?"

I looked back at the floodlights of the mall and then tranced back into her eyes. I stared and stared at her pretty face, her eyes, the stars and Venus that made her shine.

"Wait, Dad," the girl said. She slid across the seat and got outside.

"You came true," I said words from so far inside, they grew.

She put her hands on me and I dropped the wishing-well pennies onto the street.

Over all the copper, she got me through the opened orange door. "Should we take him to the hospital?"

"I'll be alright," I told her. I looked out the windshield at what lay ahead, then I looked at her, to make sure that little planet star of light would keep her real.

For the first time it felt, I woke up in daylight. My shades were open and all that warm glow poured into my room. Last week, I never would have believed it could be like this. I was laughing a lot more. I put on my new clothes and went to the record player.

Music waltzed out and I smiled like a tangerine. Soon, in only an hour, Lena Palomino would be near. Her father was bringing her here in his tow truck, to take us to the park for a walk. The girl I wished on Venus for. I had to laugh at the fate of it.

The shoe started bouncing against my window glass. The long string swung it madly like a pendulum.

I let my music play.

I went to the window and opened it up. Catching the shoe as it came at me again, I pulled down as hard as I could.

Someone above yelped and tumbled out, flashing past me on the way into a shrub underneath.

I shut my window on that sight—too many days I'd put up with him and now he could flail in the branches for as long as it took an apple to ripen and land on the ground.

For the first time in my life it seemed, I sat down in my chair by the bright glass of day to enjoy music, to happily watch the way the sun changed everything it touched.

WHITE RUSSIA

I was lonely as a tunnel. Birds flew from me.
And night invaded me with her powerful army.
To survive I forged you like a weapon,
like an arrow for my bow, or a stone for my sling.

—Pablo Neruda

1.

I was on the billboard putting up another sign when I heard the news. The girl I work with carries a radio. I stopped working, put the stack of letters by my feet and sighed. Not that I was taken by surprise—I know it happens to everyone sooner or later. Still, there was nothing I could say in reply. I just stared at the roofs and trees. My number had been read.

When the music came back on, Peg said, "Hey!" over the sound. Her side of the billboard was filled with words and she was waiting for me to catch up.

I picked up my letters and quickly patched them to the surface of the billboard, while she listened to the radio and smoked a cigarette. In a couple minutes, she flicked the spent cigarette at a yard below. Then she read out loud the thirty foot sentence we had written:

Good News!
You will have an unexpected treasure.

I don't usually pay any attention to the fortunes we display by the hundreds all over the skyline. It's just propaganda for the war. It must have been the way she said it that woke me up. Looking at the rows of houses and stores sewn together with ancient wires and trees for shadows, I began to believe that no matter how bad it might seem, a treasure really was waiting for me.

2.

We climbed down the ladder to the ground. Peg descended with music. She turned the radio off after we collapsed the ladder and pushed it back on the truck. A dog was barking at us from the other side of a wooden fence.

"That's all for today," Peg said.

We got in the truck and she started the electric engine. She was always in a hurry. The truck almost speared a mailbox as we shot down the green neighborhood street. "What a place to put a mailbox!" she said in response. It felt like we rolled up on two wheels as the truck shuddered into a new street. "Why you being so quiet?" she asked me.

I loosened my hand on the plastic dashboard. "I…" I began, but suddenly I threw my hands in front of my face.

Our truck braked against a row of shredded hawthorn, weeds and berry vines. Black army transports grinded past us. Inside their thick metal walls, you knew the new batch of youths were being sent to the war. Blue smoke was left burning in the air, the ground shook, and then they were gone.

3.

Peg drove slowly the rest of the way to the office. We listened to songs on the radio. I couldn't speak either. The sight of the army and the fear had returned.

We parked in front of the old factory and got out. The darkening sky pushed the smoke back from the brick chimneys. Along the roof ran cold alphabet. The neon letters of The Fortune Company have been turned off for years because of the war. I bet it was a beautiful sight to see them before, shining with the stars at night. I wonder about those days you see in photographs, with people wandering in a city full of lights. Now it's almost forgotten…For fear of rockets, every light must be hidden when the sun goes down.

Peg opened the door with her password and we went inside the building.

The night manager, Benny Fritz, was waiting. His back leaned against a filing cabinet. He flapped a blue card in his hand expectantly.

"Lewis," he said. "Your number got called." He held my card almost happily.

I felt Peg grab my arm.

I couldn't look at them. I looked at my shaking hand.

"Drafted," Benny said expansively, as his arm bloomed out dramatically. "And it's reassuring to know that soon you'll be fighting for our side."

4.

This is where my sadness lies. When you get close to someone, the war can take them away forever. I've seen it happen over and over and it's made me scared of living and so full of sorrow. When I think of it, I become absolutely hollow. I close myself as if a shadow lives in me and the light doesn't even know how to get back in.

Peg caught up with me as I walked across the black pavement. "Lewis! Why didn't you tell me?" I caught the hysteria in her eyes. She seized me. She didn't have the radio playing. "What are you going to do?"

"I don't know," I said. I didn't. I couldn't concentrate. I felt like I was on a conveyor belt, moving with machinery parts. I must have looked pretty hopeless.

Her voice got lower, "Okay…I can help you." There weren't any street lights. I could only look at the impression of her shaped against the buildings. "You don't have to give up. Follow me."

5.

There are some good things about the nighttime city without lights. We saw a white owl perched on a rusted lamppost. His head swiveled to watch us cross the street. It feels like a black forest made of tall building trees. Peg and I stopped in a kind of field, striped weeds and puzzles of broken metal, looking out at the slow moving river. Moon and starlight glittered upon it and swirled.

Peg took my arm, "You will need papers. They will prove that you can't go to war." I could see her smile rising with the conspiracy, "Maybe there's something out of the ordinary with you? You're not like other people, are you? Maybe your sight isn't so good? What if you see only a blur? Or is something else wrong? The right words on your papers can keep you here."

6.

That night, I couldn't sleep. My eyes went restlessly back and forth between the birdhouses and the pictures glowing in faint colors on my walls. Peg had taken my papers to be counterfeited. I could picture some ogre underground with a microscope, paint and ink, knives and paper, squinting and changing my story. I tossed and looked back at the clock. It was 2:57. Even if I could dream, what would it be?

Finally, I turned on the tin, battery powered reading candle. The soft lightbulb showed my bed's raked lines of shadows. There was an open book on the blankets. I moved to its ragged leaves to read. Only a few sentences tried and failed to catch me—the book was sleeping and wanted me to be too. So I turned the candle off and tried again.

The phosphorous pictures on the walls brightened. They were the saints from long ago, wearing starry robes, holding children and animals and relics with smoky Italian hills and clouds in the background. Between two birdhouses, I concentrated on Saint Francis until he, or me, or both of us, faded to become the darkness of sleep.

7.

The morning streets clatter with bicycles of everyone going to work. There are horses pulling carts full of vegetables, or furniture and parts. A few electric trucks buzz along. To avoid all the traffic, I turned down a side street.

The birches and willows bending overhead are starting to turn green with spring. I saw someone pulling up their blackout shade, yawning. A singing holly tree is filled with sparrows and starlings. There's a woman in her Victory Garden planting out a row of tomatoes.

All of it seems so far away from war. But that's all I can think about. Peg told me we could get my papers sometime today. That's really all I can see as I ride past the houses and trees.

The street slopes towards the river.

I stopped pedaling and coasted. I could see the morning water sparkling and the bridge padded with gray sandbags. I steered out of the green street, onto the avenue. It's funny to ride among so many bicycles, all of us rustling like leaves.

I always stop in the center of the bridge to lean over the metal and sandbags to watch the current for a while. Pigeons swerve from the bolted arches, in the water flotsam schools like fish. I see a red colored tree washing underneath. It's all around, wanting to stay calm, the city shouldn't be at war.

8.

Getting to work, Peg was waiting for me on the plastic hood of our electric truck. Clasped to her belt, the radio played, while she fumbled her hand in the orange pocket of her coat. I thought it was a cigarette she was looking for, but she pulled out a bent crust of bread and threw it to a crow.

The bird pecked it up and flew to the corner of the roof. Three flying machines edged along the horizon. People went in through the silver entrance of Fortune.

I turned and saw Peg put her finger to her lips, as she slid off the hood and opened the truck door. Letters were poured on the seat and floor. She kicked them aside and sat down.

I got in too, almost afraid to ask.

Spinning the wheel and purring us out of the parking lot, she promised me, "After work I'll take you somewhere."

9.

The city ran below us. Its banks were littered with cans and half buried rubber tires and other garbage. The water was turned copper from the leaking factories. Some yellow weeds, like giraffes, bent trying to sip from the stream.

We were adding another fortune to the air so the crumbled tenements can see that their day holds promise. The black windows point this way. How many of their children have disappeared? And what can we do to console, but give them hopeful words.

Peg leaned back to loudly read the new billboard, "You are learning more every day."

I gathered the paste and brushes and loaded them into buckets. The wind flew up with the smell of cherry blossom. I breathed deeply. It could have knocked me down.

Unfolding a map in the wake of the flower breeze, Peg searched for the flapping creased paper. She looked beyond the tenements, to a spot a square mile away. "That's our next sign."

I looked to where she pointed, but my eyes stopped on a rooftop instead. I thought it was a Chinese parade dragon—trousers, shirts and dresses, tangling and kicking on their clothesline.

10.

    With my new papers, I believe I could leave this city, hop a train and disappear. I'd take care of myself on the run. I wouldn't have to be a part of it anymore. They can't figure out what they're doing to the world. Let them war until the loss of blood finally stops them drained, because another America deserves a chance.

    Already it's changed so much since I was a child. I remember and compare. One pair of eyes has seen this. Just by watching and knowing. Maybe I could do more. If only I weren't so sad with loss. That's what gets me defeated. It's such a tide passing. I feel I could fill another river with it.

    "We're almost there," Peg said, startling me.

    The trolley rocked. It was full of people. I was looking over some woman's shoulder at the evening river as we crawled along, pulled by six horses. When they slowed to a stop, Peg took my hand and led me to the door.

    Back on the worn street, the trolley chimed away from us. Bicycles weaved their own paths and we fell in with the sidewalk crowd.

    Peg tapped my arm, "Don't look so afraid. You're almost there." Laughing, she was quoting another fortune we planted today, over in the field by the broken down railroad tracks.

    "You're right," I smiled, so wanting to believe. It's odd that it's my job to say such hope with authority when really I feel the opposite. The store windows reflected a girl walking a balloon, dragging it on the ground.

    A door opened and before I even read the number on it, Peg pushed me inside.

    Dimly lit by oil lamps, at first I thought

the walls were covered by butterflies. No, when I looked closer, I saw they were maps, folded and pinned in ways to resemble wings. The whole colored world is pictured this way. I was amazed…To think a room like this existed, hidden from the rest of the city.

I followed an ocean from the shuddered window. It bent and became a desert, then fanned into the words *Romania*, in old-style print. That land folded to the mouth of the Amazon, which twisted like an artery further along the wall. I looked up for a moment to see constellations lit up on blue paper. Someone created the world to be joined, each a part of something else that gave it life.

I walked around the world until I arrived back where Peg waited to introduce me.

11.

"This is Lewis Thread," she said. And she told me, "This is Bella Mars."

Then Peg and the world disappeared. I've never been so aware of words. I was looking up at the stars on the ceiling trying to find what to say. "Did you put these walls together?"

Bella smiled, "Yes."

Oh, her eyes were there. I could tell we were known to each other.

"I love maps," she laughed. "I filled the store with them."

I was changing so fast into someone else that I could barely think. I know it happens this way. I was afraid to look too long into her eyes.

"I finished your papers," she said. She pushed a map across the counter. "Inside here."

My hands reached and touched her fingers holding it before they went back to her sides. I looked at her, then down to the map. "Atlantis?" I brought it close to study. "I didn't know Atlantis was a real place?"

Bella laughed and didn't say anything but watch me.

I answered myself, "I guess you could say that about almost anywhere." My eyes turned to her quickly.

"You can look at them," she told me.

The seashell colors of the map held my papers underneath where nobody could see.

"I gave you a bad heart," Bella said and laughed. "That ought to fool them."

12.

It began to rain in the late afternoon as Peg and I were climbing down.

Now our billboards were quoting Emily Dickinson. The giant letters of the fortune gleamed like the title of a wet, silent movie.

Spring rain is warmer than the air. I stood on the softened ground, facing up at the gray white clouds with a smile and my eyes closed. In my mind was the obvious—Bella had been growing and growing since yesterday when I left the map store. Now she was sunflower-sized inside of me.

"Lewis!" Peg started to laugh. She pointed at the billboard and I opened my eyes to read it.

Bella is the thing with feathers.

In a dream, I had changed the poet's word, Hope, into Bella. All my thoughts all day had finally been spelled out for the whole wishing city to see. Huge letters in the rainy sky.

13.

Rain was pouring around me in the intersection where I ran, dodged a rickshaw and a horse-drawn carriage. A motorcycle circled me. I jumped out of the way and landed on the old monorail track. I hurried across to the sidewalk. Stores were protected by umbrellas that hung over me and the crowd, water splashing on the scene like the return of Atlantis.

From the wash of gutters against the bricks, the smallest man, wearing a prism suit and a gold top hat approached me and held up his tiny hand. Without a word, he gave me two slips of narrow paper, then he turned into the crowd of legs and he vanished.

The ink on the tickets blurred from the heavy drops of rain, almost running the words like tears. I read it. I thought about it. A plan occurred to me. I put the tickets into my coat pocket and I chose another street.

14.

The world flattened into wallpaper lit by candles. The room had the air of a French cathedral falling more and more into night, as we blew out the light. Finally, in darkness, Bella found me and took my hand. Her warm fingers touched over my wrists in a healing fit.

Out the door, into the moonlit street where the big drops of rain hit and splashed silver. She locked the store with a medieval key. She smiled at me again and took a map of Mexico from her bag. Mexico was large enough to hold over our heads so we could stay dry.

We walked close together, next to the stream the street had become. Carts were parked next to the curb. We stopped at one to buy food. The water beaded diamonds on the terraces of fruit. We picked apples and pears. I paid the woman with ration cards while Bella held the map up over us. A donkey pulling a cart paddlewheeled past. The air drifted the smell of flowers and river, with radios playing for the vendors.

15.

Under the city, a whole different city moves. It steams through the manhole covers. It rumbles in the old subway tunnels. As the sun collapses, pulling a cover of night over the blacked-out factories and apartments, beneath the streets, the catacombs come to life with their own daylight made from a thousand candles and lamps.

Bella hooked her arm through mine and we went down the steps.

Wicks burned in the perched stainglass bowls that led us to the cobblestoned landing below. A painted wooden sign was surrounded by all sizes of melting white candles.

"Saturn Circus," Bella read softly. Her rainy hair touched my skin. We could hear calliope threading and echoing from not far away. A pack of children ran around Bella and me, their cheers and laughing dreamily sent rattling.

A man appeared before us magically, dressed as a giant, clacking on stilts. His hat brushed the ceiling, his long shadow spider webbed the rounded ceiling and floor. "Good evening, good evening," he nodded, ladder height, "The Saturn Circus is only a footsteps journey." His striped arm shined out with a lantern to point the direction.

16.

Two chairs waited under the stone archway facing a golden curtain made sparkling from paraffin spotlights lined in front. Bella and I sat down.

She took an apple from her pocket and gave it to me. I rubbed the yellow skin on my sleeve and let her take the first bite. "Mr. Thread," she smiled, my sweetheart cupping the apple in her hands. Gold charms sparked on the soft of her neck. I touched her cheek, followed the curve to her ear. Her eyes were wide and pretty as a forest doe. I whispered her name too.

A xylophone of bells began to play a misty nursery rhyme and along the curtain edges entered wooden puppets. One by one in their slow dance from the black lying beyond. Just as the scene began to reveal, Bella passed me the apple.

17.

Fireflies scattered chaotic circles in the universe black. The constellations kept changing shapes. At last they began to form into a slow whorl. Bella rested her head on my shoulder and along my side I could feel her breathing.

The stars glowed into one light that like the sun shined into a new day given birth. We heard the bird songs on that earth. The darkness around us gave way to an orange green dawn underground. Such a beautiful moment I've never known. As Bella turned her face from the circus to me, I felt like…then suddenly the stage splashed with a fanfare.

A ten foot woman stood among the leaves and flowers of the garden. She had the shadowy silver tone of a person in a quiet film. She uncovered her eyes to stare at the ground, the mossy cobblestones planted with ferns.

In the air, a whistling was getting louder. Expecting it was part of the show, before we could react, an explosion crashed into us. In the flash, the ceiling collapsed and everything was ripped apart.

18.

I was half buried in bricks and dust. I shook my head and breathed the smoky air and coughed. People were running across the rubble with candles. They heard my cry and swarmed around me, hurrying to dig me out.

"There's someone else!" I heard myself say. I fought their arms off to stumble on hands and knees on the shifting wreck of catacombs.

By some miracle, Bella ran through the crowd and threw herself around me. We became a statue, holding each other so strongly. Really, she was the only thing that meant anything to me.

I opened my eyes once to see the precious dark of her hair, the purple sky lit by a flash of lightning. Buildings were on fire. Shadowy people ran and dragged their sirens and candles. I closed my eyes and sighed into her. I said, "I will never leave you for anything."

19.

There was a bench where I pet her sleeping back until the dawn. I made sure the sky retired the moon, when things could be seen by the Eastern slant of gray blue light. Firebells were still ringing now and then around the courtyard we had found.

Sweet Bella stirred. Her arms tightened around my waist, so I sang for her. The morning couldn't begin without someone singing (the starlings and robins were too afraid) so it was me not the birds making a melody out of the hopeful fortunes I had spelled for so many days.

She woke and stretched her legs across the bench. I noticed her heavy black boots and I smiled, "Do you always sleep with your shoes on?"

She looked around her. We were in the cavern of a torn-out building. Steeples of broken red bricks, walls slid in heaps, mixed with chairs, smashed wood, plastic, cloth and colors.

"A bomb went off," I told her quietly. "That's all I know. We are safe. I wanted to let you sleep."

Her eyes glided back to me. Happily, they closed slowly and opened again as if our being so close together was to behold a magic act.

20.

We came out of the crater effects of the bomb. A maple tree cradled new branches full of green buds where we stopped and looked down the hill. The scrambled concrete, copper and water pipes snapped and crying, ghostly wandering smoke. Horses drew the firemen's carriages. Our hips were pressed to each other. We watched silently for a while.

The war has come here, I realized. Listen… Now I must decide…To me, Bella is life. The soft dark crown of her hair on my lips is my future too. As long as we're in this place, it must be made safe.

Bella turned away from the destruction and she pulled me forward onto the first street that wasn't buckled or scarred.

In time, the street led to the globe suspended over the pavement, where the windows of her store were curtained with maps. She reached under a clay flowerpot for the front door key. It opened, we went inside, and we shut the door behind us.

21.

The city is a guitar without strings. The birds have gone, scared off by the bombing. I didn't see a single one as I traveled from Bella's to my job. It's as if the sky opened up and hid them away.

I hitched a ride with a silent rag collector who drove his plodding old horse down the middle of the street. I hopped off two blocks from The Fortune Company.

It was still early, not yet eight o'clock. I thought maybe I could have some coffee in the break room before Peg and I drove out for the day. I felt buzzing from no sleep. Each step I took was almost unreal.

Around the factory the air hummed, but when I opened the door, a wave of machinery blasted. Thousands of little white fortunes were pouring out of the printing presses. It was like a tickertape parade.

I could see Benny agitating along the assembly line. His suit was stuffed with fortunes like a straw filled scarecrow. I never saw him in such a state of panic.

"Lewis!" Peg rushed across the floor to me. "What happened to you?"

I guess I hadn't noticed. My clothes were burned and torn. I told them Bella and I were in the catacombs where the bomb hit.

Benny appeared next to us. His clipboard was piled with a mound of fortunes and they fell off him like snow. "We got a busy day. You two better leave right now." He passed Peg a list. "People are really going to need our work today."

He turned towards the machines then he stopped. "Oh, Lewis…You might want to stop at

a cobbler when you're done."
My shoes looked like alligators.

22.

The platform of our billboard slanted and bent and yesterday's paper message was nearly burned off. The edge of the bomb crater tossed up the cement into big fish shapes below us. Water flowed out of broken pipes sunk in the catacombs. There was no music on the radio, only news bulletins. So we worked in the near silence of the breeze.

Peg began to peel off the old paper skin.

My arms were full with William Blake letters. I stacked them on the platform where they wouldn't slide off, then I climbed down for the fresh paper.

Gray torn pieces of the old fortune spiraled like falling sky onto the ground. With the roll of paper slung over my shoulder, I went up rung by rung.

Halfway, I heard a bird and I almost fell off in surprise. I clung to the roll and stared where the noise chirped.

A little girl whistled through a toy in her hands. She stared up at me. Then she stopped playing it and turned a key on the toy's back. It sprouted bright yellow wings. It was chirping by itself, as it tested the air. It flew from her, glinting and singing its mechanical charm out over the ruins.

I watched it fly in clicking gasps. A bird from another world.

When it was only a dot, I looked back at the girl and realized I had been wrong.

She was a grown woman, only a few feet tall though. She didn't move. She stood there while the flaps of our billboard paper hit the rubble.

After waiting a minute or so, the metal songbird returned to her and folded back into a toy.

23.

Not many people were walking along the boulevard and those who were walked in a hurry like me. A curfew would be falling soon as it was dark, and I had to see Bella before that happened.

This day all anyone talked about was the bomb and how more would be exploding. I saw a mother running with her crying baby. I felt safer when I walked next to a Clydesdale pulling a cart full of sandbags.

The map store finally formed and I ran across the street. I couldn't wait to see her. The blinds were still up, so she must be there. Candles showed in the windows.

I opened the door in such a rush she looked up ready to scream.

"Lewis!"

In the seconds it took me to shut the door, she met me next to Egypt.

"Thank you for staying safe," I told her.

"Thank you too," she said.

When we held each other a little apart, she laughed, "Your shoes…" and I wiggled my toes for her.

The alligator mouths had opened all the way.

24.

When the curfew shut down the entire city, we locked the door, hid the windows with maps and sat together in a worn velvet chair beside a single candle light.

I said today's William Blake fortune, "Father, O Father, what do we here, in this land of unbelief and fear? The land of dreams is better far, above the light of the morning star."

She was already sleeping though. I smiled and rested my head on hers. I listened through the shrill quiet of the night surrounding us, trying to catch the sound of her dreams. They would sound like the radio. Was she on a pool of water in a map paper boat? Did the moon wear the face of the Cheshire Cat and blow the sails? I could almost hear them…A music box creak, or an old phonograph scratch.

Breathing her hair, I heard a chime that opened my eyes. I stared at the window.

The terrible silence of outside was creeping with a new sound. I recognized the calliope music. The window began to rattle, only a tremble, no more than a turtle walking across. Silhouettes of fantastic shapes marched along the shades, carrying lantern glows with their circus melody.

I didn't wake Bella because it was so nice holding her. Maybe I was dreaming anyway. I just held her. The calliope faded. I listened to the soft movement of her sleeping and then I closed my eyes too.

25.

Water clung in skirts to the air and the falling cherry flower blossoms looked like snow blowing on the street. Winter had a hard time leaving for spring. It must possess hundreds of cold hands that cling to metal signs, hold around trees and scrape fingernails in the wind down walls.

I'm not as cold as I could be though—Bella insisted that I wear her sweater. As I stumbled in the winter April morning, I thought of her, holding her hand walking with me. I stopped at a cart to buy an apple and a slice of bread.

"It's good to see you weren't scared away by the war," I said to the woman.

"Where else am I going to go?" She put the food in my hands. True, the sides of the street were parked with other vendor carts too.

I nodded my thanks and ate my breakfast as I walked. We could all survive on hope, on going about our day to day, by not being afraid. Because really, I don't want it to end, I thought of Bella Mars.

26.

By chance, I looked down an alley that was carved between the two serpent-colored walls of warehouses. Strewn with the litter of broken and rotten things, snapped ribs of pallets, I stopped when I saw half an elephant appear.

Its tail flicked and as it took a step backwards more of it showed. There were boxes and bags piled over its back, spilling fruit and vegetables when it moved.

I left the street and entered the shadows. The noise of the elephant's gray shuffling scraped on the asphalt. I walked slowly just in case I had to turn and run. I've only seen elephants in picture books, or on movie screens. They seem gentle, but how would I know? I edged around the giant weight of it and I stopped in surprise again.

A patchwork clown held a branch full of green leaves out to it, hoping to lure it into a hole in the wall. The clown pantomimed and swayed eagerly.

I watched the act going nowhere and then I asked, "Can I help?"

The clown beamed at me and motioned silently how I should push. I've never pushed an elephant. Nervously, I put my hand on its skin. I felt the solid shape resisting me. Even so, the clown tried waving the leaves again. I joined in leaning my strength for all it was worth.

The elephant began to move. I could feel the slow impulse like a Civil War train. Sunlight slipped off its back as the elephant went foot by foot into the sloping darkness. I kept pushing until it was gone. I dropped back from the shadows. I'd rather stay outside.

27.

My alligator feet yawned on the concrete. Past the wall I could hear the dull footsteps of the elephant going further underground.

Strange that the Saturn Circus is still in the catacombs…I'm surprised they didn't hitch all their cages and carriages together and leave the city at once. It seems like they should be set up in a field far away from here. I wondered why they were still here?

I was thinking of reasons (Maybe the giraffe is sick? Maybe the acrobats are searching for the gypsy's lost crystal ball?) when the street took me around the corner to the start of the wide Fortune Company parking lot.

In the distance, a ladder was set up against a tall post and a billboard leaned in the arms of twenty people. The tiny round spot of Benny berserked. His voice piped out orders to the wobbling billboard ascending the top of the pole.

The message was plain. I could read it across the distance. Black letters on a white background:

> *Help is on the way. Read your fortune*
> *every day.*

Benny directed them, hanging a museum painting in the blue sky. It tipped up to the left, went unsteadily to the right, then he shouted and froze his arms when it was level.

By the time I arrived, the billboard was being sewn into place. It reflected the early morning sun.

Benny seemed to have relaxed a little. His hands were resting on his hips while he stared up at the white. He noticed my presence and nodded towards the factory. "There's someone waiting to see you in there."

28.

It looked like a fire was coming from the black suit. There was a briefcase resting flat on his lap with a crystal ashtray burning two cigarettes. He puffed nervously on a third one, clouding the air around his face. Somehow he knew through the cloud that I had arrived.

"Mr. Thread?" He started to rise, caught the sliding ashtray and put it carefully onto the chair beside him. His expression was hidden behind black glasses. A calm dog lay at his feet.

I said, "Yes."

"I'm Mort Frixon. I'm from the government." He sat down again, unlatching his briefcase to reveal a fan of paper. "Now…We received a status report on your draft availability." He held a page. The cigarette burned so close to it I was sure it would catch aflame. "Says you got a bad heart…"

I didn't know what to say. I looked at him and waited for what was next.

"This would hurt in battle, of course. We couldn't count on you when bullets are flying. But there are so many other things you can do for our military effort. There's no reason for you to be left out. Look at me," he pointed at himself, "I'm blind."

I stared as he replaced my page in the briefcase. It was over just like that. The latches snapped locked. He concluded, "You seem perfectly capable to me."

He stood up and the service dog with him wobbled onto its three legs. "We'll see what we can find for you to do. I'll be waiting for you tomorrow."

29.

My thoughts were forgotten in the day that played out anyway. When I looked at the sky, it was that warm summer blue with a few spirit-like clouds. It looked like those clouds weren't even moving. For a moment I thought they were painted. I knew that wasn't true. I waited until my eyes caught their pulse against the still maple branches. I breathed, stopped the swelling tears, breathed again and felt the life in the air.

A bumblebee bounced across the whiteness of the new layered billboard. We still had to put the letters on, though staring at that blank shape I just couldn't picture what it could mean. Peg started to explain with her half of the sentence, but I just couldn't.

"Lewis. What's the matter?"

My mind was torn up, so I told her, "I don't know what to say. I'm being sent to war."

30.

The rest of the day, all I could do was stare at puddles as they filled with round silver drops of rain. When we climbed down from our last billboard that day, I told Peg I was walking home.

The bamboo roofs of Chinatown beat like dull piano keys. I didn't have an umbrella or newspaper or map to hold over my head. The water soaked through me, changing Bella's green sweater into a wraparound lake. Of course my shoes drank every step I took.

Across the street, a troop of boys were led along the sidewalk by Mort Frixon and his seeing-eye dog. He puffed in front of them, pulling them captured in tow. I stopped and hid and watched them trudge out of sight. Tomorrow it would be me.

I couldn't go see Bella. I didn't want her to know that I would be taken away from her too. Maybe she would just think she had dreamed me. How could I look into her beautiful face and tell her such an awful thing. It would be the worst thing in the world.

Windows were being covered as people shut themselves in for curfew.

I made it home dripping rain, pushed at the heavy, half-rotten wooden door, and went in. The hallway was lined with filling buckets. Each one pinged with water dripping from leaks.

By the scant light of blue candles and submarine sounds, I took the knotted handrail up the flight of melting stairs. I was so tired when I got to my little room, I collapsed on the bed. Before I could tell where the two worlds began and ended, I was in a dream.

31.

The window slid open. The cool lilac blue sky crawled on me. The room filled with the sound of birds I haven't heard for days. I sat up. Shadows flocked to my birdhouses to perch on the walls.

On the other side of the window, the fire escape rattled. A woman wearing a thin veil of black lace looked in. Copper bells on her clothes shook as she leaned through, smiling a face printed with tattoos. She offered her hand and I reached across the covers to take it.

I moved as the fog does. I was floated out onto the fire escape where I hovered in the slight rain. She pressed her fingers to my temples. I watched her expression concentrated on me as if she was reading. Sadness and joy showed on her face. My life written inside of me. I felt her there, knowing everything. I became afraid that she was judging me, that she might fling me off to the street, but I couldn't move. Whatever was happening to me, I wished more than anything to see Bella. Imagine never holding her again? What was I thinking? This can't be my last day.

The cloud I was on began to shake as I struggled to wake from the gypsy. Her eyelids opened and there were two golden stars. Her tattooed face became a final smile as she promised, "You won't have to worry, Lewis Thread. You are protected."

With the birds retreating overhead, she faded back into the air, leaving me out in the weather and someone else was calling my name.

32.

"Lewis?" she said. "Where are you?" As a silhouette, Bella came to the window sill and discovered me on the warped metal platform slats, waking up mysteriously.

Her arms reached for me. The spring leaves were almost crushed out of her voice, "Lewis."

I don't know how I dreamed my way out onto the fire escape.

Already the haunting was fading.

It was dawn.

"Bella." I got up to embrace her. I was shivering. I was rained on. She held me so tightly the water ran from me.

"What are you doing out here? I've been looking everywhere for you."

Bella's hands never left me as I crawled over the open window into the shaded room.

"You're soaked," she whispered. We loosened the wet buttons from me. With her own clothes, she dried me. Her shirt and skirt fell off and our skin was together, wonderful, for her warm body made me as warm as her.

I told her the obvious, that day is day and night is night, "Bella, I love you."

Lovers we are, moved to the bed where we lay down across the blankets with the little white and blue feathers that the birds left for us.

33.

When I woke up, there were arms around me. The window was filled with silver color. This morning waited for so long to appear. I breathe and my sides breathe with her. Bella's eyelashes seal her in sleep. Such a pretty face…I'm so glad, I sighed and thanked sweet life. So surprised to know I'm not dreaming, I moved my hand to brush her hair.

That made her stir. She moved her leg between mine and pressed herself to me. Dear Bella.

I want to hold her forever, but this is the day I was afraid of. I rubbed her back. I'm not scared. Somehow I know I'll stay alive. I feel it's been promised to me. The war will crash at me, but I'll not be hurt.

A bird started to sing. The chirps floated into the air in search among all the tired leaves. I knew that song's feeling and I smiled as I held Bella. The bird kept singing. I know another bird will answer him soon. That's how it happens. And so warm and tired, I fell asleep again.

34.

I was asleep in the curve of her when she woke me. She was so nice I tried to ignore the noise of the barking dog outside. The dog acted like the whole world was on fire.

Bella leaned over me and peered out the window. Quickly shying from the glass, she warned me, "There's some man out there looking up here." She was so frightened. I kissed her mouth. Holding her hands, I turned to look.

As frozen as a black park statue, Mort Frixon stood below. Suddenly his three-legged dog stopped barking and I could see the thin smile grow on Mort's face.

"Lewis Thread," he exhaled a cloud of dragon smoke. Like the grim reaper, he waited for me, casting a long blue morning shadow.

Bella moved along my back and looked over my shoulder. "Who is it?"

My call to war. The moment had arrived, though I wasn't afraid. There was the warm soft breathing of Bella with me and the words from somewhere, "You are protected…"

"Lewis Thread," the blind man repeated.

I told him, "I'll be there."

I closed the patchwork curtains. Bella kneeled on the mattress facing me. So lovely in the morning light, her pretty eyes brimmed with tears. "Don't worry darling." I gave her a chain of kisses. "Sweetheart," I held her tight, "I won't get hurt."

35.

We were paraded on the street just like the captives I saw yesterday. I was tied to someone in front of me and the rope tangled around me and continued down the line. Mort Frixon and his dog led us slowly along, lighting cigarettes, stopping at doors to add to our procession.

I didn't think about where we were going, only Bella stayed with me. I had left her wrapped in a white flannel sheet. Don't cry, I begged her and brushed under her eyes. I needed to think of her safe in her store, with the beautiful world all around. That's all I want to think about until I return.

When we stopped marching, we were lined up in a row. Barbed wire formed a tall square wall enclosing us. Mort Frixon hobbled to the place his dog found for him.

I didn't listen to his speech. Why not let him think he's captured me and we are his for the war. I know this is only something I'll pass through. The war can't last long. I'll return soon and wake every morning with Bella for the rest of my life.

A soldier walked in front of me and took me away from the rest of the line. I was escorted through a gate, out of the barbed wire.

I'm sure I can't be hurt. You can't be hurt when you're in a dream. You always wake up before that moment.

36.

The city showed me its blue outlined buildings. The sparkled lights were going out for curfew…Bella too. She must be finishing the day beside yellow candles.

The truck jumped as it followed the road, shaking us, and when I looked out the back again, the city was gone. I saw trees lacing over the sky. A half-moon ran along.

I don't know where we're going. None of us do. We've been examined, stamped and given this new life. There's a number sewn on my uniform—that's who they named me. We were all very quiet with our thoughts. Tired enough after a long day with the military, but nobody's asleep, eyes avoid each other.

An hour or more might have passed. Then the engine's steady noise changed when the driver broke gears and stopped. We all fell out of our thoughts.

We heard the door up front open and slam shut, followed by footsteps approaching us.

His shape there in the dark called out numbers, snapping out those around me. So quickly some of us were gone. Then the engine started and we traveled on.

37.

It was early dawn when we arrived to a stop where cool wind blew inside the truck. Only a few of us were left, all the rest were scattered away. Again those footsteps and that man came to call numbers.

We listened. We heard wind and what sounded like thunder. The gray colored man said only one thing: that was me.

I lifted myself, a hand touched my shoulder for luck, and I went out the end of the truck and landed on the ground.

I smelled the ocean. The surf was what the thunder had been, waves crashing at the Pacific sand. I must be meant for right on the edge of the sea. I was handed a thick envelope while I stood there. Then the truck started to roll without me, leaving me alone in this place of dunes and reeds.

I listened to that engine get distant into the sound of surf. When they were gone, I still didn't dare move. I tore open my instructions.

My orders directed me in words I could barely read, to go straight ahead. Against the sky, I could see a tower. It wasn't far away. And a path made from broken shells led to it.

38.

Yesterday I woke in Bella's arms and legs. This morning I'm on a sandy covered wooden floor in a glass walled lookout tower. Windows make a glass square over me, a kaleidoscope of blue sky and white drifts of clouds.

This is your war, the directions said. My orders printed on the paper: *Watch for Rockets…*

A powerful telescope slanted against the glass.

I'm really living in the air, a part of the air, a hundred feet off the ground, above the sea.

I sat up and yawned. Curious seagulls glide in the current around my tower. The sky looks the way it should. But if I happen to see a white contrail emergency, there's a radio for me to call Mayday. Keeping the radio company was a hotplate with a pan and a stack of silver ration cans. It's a simple thing I need to do: watch the sky, be the eyes that make sure we are safe from death.

39.

In the late afternoon, I went through the trapdoor in the floor, climbed down the long ladder onto the sand. I went for a walk close to the foamy shifting pattern of ocean waves.

It's impossible to stare at the sky all the time. I needed this pause to chase the terns and sandpipers running along the shore. Driftwood and broken shells shined in the wet sand. My footsteps were left on the beach.

It's beautiful out here. When I breathe in the deep sea air, I wish I had Bella's hand I mine. Talking to myself, I spoke to her. I say, "Look at that rock out there. Doesn't it look like a seal charging the waves? Don't you love the sun on the water in a hundred orange pieces? If you picked up all those patches, you could fit them into a hot round circle. Look at the cormorants, drying their wings like black swans. We can spell magic words in the sand for the mermaids to pull away. Do you think the ocean is a blanket for the sleeping land? Could a starfish and a flower hold each other? The waves have Japanese poems in them. Or that silver curl might be an Asian fortune sent from Lao Tzu, collapsing here on America."

With the one you love forever, you can imagine anything. The pages of a book open perfectly, one after another, to the two of us. And it's clear where I stand in the war, Lewis Thread on this curve of endless blue splashing, missing my dear Bella Mars.

40.

By nightfall, clouds bringing rain turned me back to the tower. Water beaded diamonds on my invisible ceiling and cried down the walls. It was impossible to watch for rockets through the storm, so I lit a candle. It flickered and cast a pen shadow across the letter I was writing.

Just think, soon your words will be going into her. She'll read you over and over again. So I wrote her many pages to be her company, until the candle melted in a white nightgown shape and I blew the flame out.

I turned over on my back to stare at the black.

The sea wind showed me how a birdhouse feels, like a cradle rocked in the trees. The tide runs its own music, hypnotic and sleepy.

I closed my eyes. Hello again, I said to the wooden dream doors that I pushed open. Beyond, rainy cobblestones revealed, but I held back from there. I had to return to the awake world.

The room began to hum louder with the rattling saw blade pitch of something passing close by in the air.

I jumped out of the cover of my sleeping bag.

Against a dark foggy swirl, I could see it.

What was it? What's that floating round black beetle shape making so much noise? There were bolts circling it, shining with rain. The thing was only a yard away, wandering like a microscope when I pushed open the window and grabbed the heaviest thing to throw—a typewriter.

41.

When the typewriter hit it, the thing cried out hurt and screeched crashing to the ground. I leaned over the frame and saw sparks flash in the sand not far below. The glow lit up the dunes.

I closed the window and put on my scattered uniform.

Opening the trapdoor, the surf crash was the only sound. It wasn't inviting. The midnight waited for me, slipping my hold on the ladder as I went into it.

Some fire still crackled ahead in the eelgrass, burning the weed tinders and wild strawberries. A coil of yellow orange white light waited.

Not sure of what I was entering, I crept warily on the sand, into the cutting blades of beach plants. Phantom trees crabbed, I could hear their leaves bristling. Just ahead of me was the source of eeriness.

Glowed by its torn sparking wires, it moved a couple steel feelers pathetically. Then it faded from life.

I didn't have a flashlight or candle to tell me what kind of thing I'd knocked from the sky. I took a few steps closer.

A very sad broken machine was outlined in the thorns.

"I'm sorry," I said. I kneeled. Before I went back to the tower to radio it in, I wanted the wet ruin to know how I felt and that I wished it to wake into a better mechanical world.

42.

As I led Mort Frixon and his dog across the heath, I was trying not to laugh.

I don't think Mort's dog has ever been to the sea before, so happy and eager the way he leaned into the leash, straining towards the ocean, in disregard of the blind man's stumbling. The white gulls in the surf lured the dog like harpies.

Mort splashed through a little swamp and paintbrushing cattails as he was dragged in a zigzag with me. Mort pulled the dog to his side as he tried to behave like he was in control. "What time did you say it flew by here?" Mort said.

"It must have been around midnight," I answered. "I'm not sure exactly though." I grabbed his arm so he didn't hit a sticker bush. Forgetting he couldn't see, I pointed, "There it is."

The flying machine was crashed ten feet from us.

"Good. Take me there."

Mort's black officer's uniform was stretched between the direction of the sea and me, edging him step by step towards the wreck.

It looked like a metal bird's egg that had fallen off a bough. I could see little gears, tubes, wires, other contraptions that jostled from its cracked open shell.

While Mort was tying his struggling dog to a stunted tree, I put my hand into the machine and took out a loose piece that had attracted my attention.

The bright plaque was stamped with tiny words, *Made in USA*. How could that be? I slipped it into my pocket to hide it from the blind man.

Mort began to run his hands over the

braided bolts. It didn't take him long to identify. "This is one of the enemy's flying spies. There's a camera inside." Bent over to search it, he threw out a fountain of parts.

I watched but I didn't understand what this meant. What was this thing really? Why was it made in America? I wanted it to make sense. I asked, "How do you know it's from the enemy?"

"They've used these before. I must have examined hundreds of them. The enemy might even send another one tonight to look for this one they lost." Deep in the machine, Mort paused, "Here it is." He ripped off the coils and brought the camera out. "The film in this can tell us what they're interested in. I'll take this back with me." He gripped my shoulder proudly. "You did a fine job, Lewis. People get medals for doing things like that."

43.

Before Mort and his dog left, he opened the camouflage hatch of his carriage and showed me three typewriters. "These are for you," he said. "Ammunition."

We took them out and set them on the sand. His dog put a wet nose to smell them, dripping a shadow of salt water.

'Thanks," I said.

Mort opened the coach door and the dog poured in. Becoming more at ease, Mort began lighting cigarettes. As the cloud formed around him, he told me, "Keep watching, Lewis. You've won a battle."

He saluted me so dramatically that I felt I had to respond the same way. The reigns snapped, the wooden wheel spokes creaked like clock hands and the brown horse left tracks in the sand.

I watched them go. Painted in my sight, they dwindled with swallows going like children swings in the air. When the carriage disappeared, I turned.

A patch of burned ground, and the remains were left like a war memorial. I had three typewriters at my feet to bring up to the tower floor, to throw if something flying should disturb my night again.

44.

One after another, I carried the typewriters away to stack on the plywood floor next to the window. The glass was blue and white. I couldn't imagine the sight of another whatever-machine. Made in America…What was going on? Was America at war with itself? Who were we fighting? In all the time it's been going on, nobody will say. How did I get caught in this? I put my hands across my eyes and sighed. I will have to figure this out for myself.

I was tired. I lay down on the floor. I watched the sky until my eyes shut, opened, shut and closed.

45.

Bella and I were in a warm place. It might have been Mexico because I heard mariachi-like wind chimes in the sunny air. She sang to me in Spanish, while the waves gradually washed away the land around us. When the sand was gone, we floated on blue water. She kept us together by sewing kelp and seaweed into a bed. She never stopped singing, though she had been turned into a mermaid and lost the ground. What she had gained was the whole world of ocean. And so did I become like her too, with a green scaled tail to swim layers if we wanted to (learning all the fish as I used to know all the birds) or to hold me with her in the orange glitter of the setting sun. That was a special surprise because when the night arrived, she was dressed in thousands of stars. We pulled that cloth over us to sleep. We were calm in love until the churning metal hum of a steam engine ship. Bella grabbed my shoulder, "Wake up!" I could see her pretty face lit by the approach of the boat. "Wake up, Lewis!" I wanted to tell her not to worry, I was with her, but the dream we were in disappeared.

46.

What woke me was the beehive sound of another flying machine. I could see its dark lurking oval slowly nearing the tower windows. So once again, just like last night, I staggered in a hurry to the glass and threw a typewriter out.

The hit didn't quite knock it from the sky. The shrill crying machine banked as it fought against the smoke that knotted out of its broken side. I heard it bump into the dunes. This one had not exploded, it could still be functioning, taking photos of the murky seashore.

I picked up a typewriter in preparation for what I might find waiting. Getting it down the steep ladder in the dark was difficult. I had to rest and catch my breath when my bare feet landed in the snowy feel of the sand.

I heard a squeak nearby. A chatter of static…

Maybe its wings were all that I hurt. With the typewriter held against my chest, I went as quietly as I could in that direction. Sharp leaves caught my legs. I walked until the machine became apparent.

It was still alive. It was brushing its ruined propeller with silver claws.

I raised the typewriter above my head, ready to crush the spy machine, when I heard a voice come from it.

Tiny, metallic sounding words came out.

Kneeling, I set the typewriter in the sand so I could get closer to the words. At first it was like listening to an anthill, then gradually I could discern what was being said.

"A change in the weather will bring you

pleasure…We were very tired, we were very merry…"

It squealed on and on.

I stopped listening. I got up off my knees. Naturally I recognized the messages. They were the very same fortunes that I've been tacking to the city billboards.

47.

The Made in America War no longer mattered to me. By the early morning light, the sounds of birds and sea, I put my letter to Bella in my coat pocket and I left the tower for good.

A long walk back to the city awaited me, but once I began moving my feet over the dirt, I started to sing.

The war is to conquer my own sorrow, loss and defeat. There was no reason for that blind Mort Frixon to own the freedom of my life, or to keep me embedded in some pointless nightmare, because I know where I need to be.

What seemed like a cloud I've been lost in, I finally passed through.

48.

I discovered that I wasn't alone. The road to the city had other soldiers like me, returning. Everyone was talking about the way they'd been used. They were saying there never would have been a war if we'd been strong enough to stay where we were. I had to agree, that was my feeling too.

We kept walking and from out of the passing woods and meadows, more soldiers joined us, until we were so many that our boots made the dust form a cloud that surely could be seen from the tops of the distant skyscraper relics. The war was over because we wanted it to be.

The walking made me thirsty. It must have been just luck or perhaps some guiding angel's touch that sent me off the road to a spring I saw.

The glade softly muffled the noise of all the soldiers. My reflection in the green surface looked at me. Cupped hands broke the mirror as I leaned to drink.

That sight of water pulled me in. I was thrown by the force of the road buckling.

49.

Sunlight and cold water brought me out of the dark. My eyelids were heavy leaves I had to rub open. I felt smooth rocks underneath me as I forced myself to sit, to see the gold and silver colored waves.

Buildings grew on the land on the other side. Bridges went across to my right and left. I recognized them though I couldn't cast my memory back to how I arrived.

Somehow I floated to the city. I felt made of seaweed as I tried to stand.

The city, river and land, whirled.

My shoes squished across the rocks in a jagged path that took me from the bank onto a grassy hill. I collapsed to my knees in the tall weeds. Bright yellow dandelions grew by the hundreds like fallen constellations.

I saw people going through the field harvesting the flowers into bags. Their painted carts and horses waited under trees.

I watched the gypsies as quietly as a broken scarecrow, for half of me felt like washed straw, until they got closer.

The bells on a woman coppered near to me and I asked her in a weak voice if she could spare me some food. My rough words came out as wind, but her deep eyes could tell by looking at me.

50.

She turned the crank on the wooden record player and let the scratchy crackle of old Caruso sing to me. She served me thick slices of rich brown bread covered with butter and she reached for a kettle hanging from a branch to pour me tea.

The music and warm food in the shade began to revive me and when she sat down, I said, "I was in the war, but not anymore."

She stared at me very carefully. "Then," she said, "You won't need that uniform."

It was dark gun metal color and soaked from the spring and the river. "Do you have any other clothes for me?"

She nodded.

While she was gone, I finished eating, set the plate in the grass and winded up the record player again. The voice came from the Victrola's cornucopia horn.

The birds over me sat in the twigs. The leaves were brushed onto the blue ocean endless sky. If I had fallen up instead of down, I would have drowned in that hot air, or shipwrecked on a cloud on a mountain top. But invisibly and fatefully, I was led here. Someone's dream promise to me was still true: I was protected.

51.

Going through the city streets now seemed like a hundred years had passed. I can't explain how different I felt.

Summer weather had arrived while I'd been away. I was grateful for the shadowy elms. Little bells of the ice cream truck, the sparrow sounds of kids playing games on the sidewalks. I didn't see any soldier uniforms. Everyone was dressed for the season, including me.

I stopped at the place where the catacombs exploded and I saw that it had all been smoothed out. The rubble had been carted away and new roses were growing beside the rebuilt entrance leading underground. Yellow ropes were spun to keep people off the seeded ground. Amazing the way it was so different from the last time I was here.

I kept walking past the open doors of stores and the animal carts. I recognized the woman who sold us apples and pears. I didn't have time to stop though, because I was so close to the world map store.

52.

Seeing its bricks, wood and glass with the sign hanging over the street spilled right out of a dream. I almost couldn't breathe, with my heart rising like a balloon.

Imagining all the ways I could go through the door had been in my thoughts for so long and now here I was. The moment was here and I ran across the last feet of street.

Inside, I laughed at how the globe curved the sunlight and the maps were flying bird wings. It felt so much like home that I almost cried. There were the birdhouses I made, set up on the counter.

But where was she?

I leaned over the counter to look. She wasn't there. Pillars of maps stacked the back of the store, almost touching the ceiling. "Bella?"

It was so quiet, I was suddenly worried. If something happened to her, what would I do? And I thought of how scared she must have been while I was in the war.

"Bella?" I spun round the pillars calling her name. Where was she? I tried to be calm.

With both hands I held a blue and green planet with all the countries painted on. I made a prayer.

I held the world to my stomach like a baby and when I looked up, in the doorway, Bella was standing there.

53.

Night made peace with the day. They passed each other going opposite ways. Bella left the screen door open so we could hear the birds, the splashy echoes and breeze.

We blew out the candles and lamps except for the one lit inside a globe. It cast the green shapes of continents on the wall.

Africa went over us in the middle of all the glow-in-the-dark ceiling stars.

We held each other wrapped in the blanket fleece. She closed my eyes and told me she knew I would be back. She knew there was something watching over me.

Finally she rested her lips to my neck. We were so warm together and we just walked right into sleep.

54.

A cottony dream was pulling apart and I opened my eyes on the brown morning skin next to me. I didn't want her to stir. It was so nice holding her.

On a Sunday morning, the robins were starting the day outside. The sun was pulleyed up over the mountains.

I watched Bella's eyes open. She kissed me before I thought of what to say.

We listened to the city birds. At this hour nothing else moves out there. I've made birdhouses they're probably singing from.

"If you were in my dream," Bella said, "Were you dreaming with me?"

I kissed her mouth, told her, "Of course."

She smiled along my lips.

Outside, we could hear the clattering sounds of horse hooves on the bricks and the concrete street. Bella sat up and we stared at the window as the first horse passed.

Their round white eyes showed their surprise at running free. They were trailing ropes from their necks. Six of them ran by.

I slid from Bella, stood up and hurried to the door to look outside. I caught sight of the horses disappearing around a corner. Following their echo, a strange still quiet reigned on the cobbled street.

The birds were silent too as Bella put herself around me again.

55.

10:30 rhymed in the harpsichord notes of the walnut clock on the wall. Like a wave, Bella rose from me. She stopped at the window and looked out the curtain. With the yellow sun on her face, she turned and held her hand out for me.

How could it be any better? She waited for me, smiling. I've sanded wood for birdhouses to almost the softness of her skin.

We held each other for every lost moment we'd been apart. The loneliness of the ocean and city…I felt her start to cry into my neck as I stroked her hair. I closed my eyes too, I felt the same way. We'll have every day from now on though.

"I have a surprise for you," I said.

"You're a surprise," she said. I watched the shape of her lips when she said it.

I touched her mouth to mine. "I want to take you somewhere. Not far away. Just put a sweater on and wear a flower."

56.

Most of the city was still quiet this late morning. We held hands, walking alleys. It moved like a movie.

Bella didn't know where I was taking her. She kept guessing and laughing. So much fun lay in this playing, but I wasn't going to tell her yet.

Whenever we found a flock of wildflowers in the cement, I pulled out a stem to add to her. She had so many petals and vines, she looked like a garden. I said, "We're almost there."

She must have sensed where our path was taking us, going past the gardens in yards, the sparrows flying off the cracked cement, a leafy blue green tree overhead. Bella's hand formed a perfect hold with mine. The whole world was a flower for her.

"We're going to the reservoir?" she finally guessed and I couldn't lie to her.

"Yes." Already the obvious dark trees on the hill were around us, tall Douglas fir and cedar. We left the last evidence of the city and sloped into the trampled weeds. Bending maples sheltered the sky into tartan patterns of yellow and blue.

"What are we going to do at the reservoir?" she asked me. I hummed a little pretend merry-go-round song and squeezed her hand.

We left the trail and stopped at the base of a tall concrete old stairway that went up steeply for a hundred feet.

As we took each step, I told her a story. "In that city you see…" I brushed the hair from her shoulder so she could see the city at our back. From this height, it twirled in the bowl of green hills below. "Down there was me, you know. For years, I was in a fairy tale curse..." I led her up another step and we kept climbing. "I was asleep in a bad dream. And the same vines you see on these trees grew on me too. Then, out of the blue…" I just stepped up the rest of the way with her, holding her, until we stopped at the top, waiting for the sight to be the words.

There was the reservoir, scooped into the hilltop. Firs grew all around the water. And Bella noticed the white ribbon tied to the fences and floating in the wind.

I let that sight tell her how I felt.

57.

By the time of twilight, we lay back in the tall grass and watched the sky. I laughed again at Bella's surprise, for now we were far above the city and we were married. Everyone has their own ceremony. We held hands around the biggest tree we could find and we asked to grow as old. There are other things we made up along the way. Bella's ideas were added to mine.

We let it last until she chose this calm mossy place to rest.

The lights in the city were staying on even though darkness was settling and starlight had come about, sparkling over us. A Ferris Wheel spiraled all colors for the people down there. Everyone was tired of the war. It had to stop.

Bella stretched in my arms, sighing wonderfully. The white ribbon tied in her hair touched my mouth. I kissed through to her. "How are you, Bella?"

"Lewis," she turned and sat up, "I think we are ready to return." She stood and I stood with her. The path showed through the grass, like a river past the reservoir and under the trees. We moved on it, drawn with the moths towards the city.

58.

I guess it had been when we were children when we last saw the city like this. There were lanterns hung from the trees, over the sidewalk and street, every house had candles in windows. There were people playing music and games. Bella and I were laughing at it all.

A girl was painting stars on everything and she didn't stop at my shoes, she went over them and down the curb onto the concrete. Another child grabbed the hem of Bella's dress and took us both along. Maybe it was a parade or a crusade.

We were the tallest in the stream, pulled by the singing, the whistling candle toys and twirling golden whirligigs. A whole jazz band was playing on the corner where we turned and fell in step behind an even larger march.

Bella drew my arm and pointed at the elephant in front of us. A small man in a tuxedo danced on its swaying back. We all gasped and clapped as a man walking alongside swallowed a torch and blew a cloud of yellow fire.

"It's the Saturn Circus!" we said.

An ostrich stopped to eat the flower off a rhododendron. The children flowed around us. A woman dressed in veils reached out her tattooed arms and touched our shoulders in a kind of blessing.

She said something I couldn't hear because of all the excitement. She smiled, catching me with a sudden dreamy feeling, and then she went into the crowd, dancing again.

59.

What a sight, to watch the circus acrobats climb up the bridge suspension wires carrying candles. While the white trick horses turned in circles, ballerinas on their backs, jugglers tossed pins and the rest of Saturn performed for us in the middle of the bridge.

It was lit overhead with candles and when the ringmaster started the elephant moving again, we all followed along, leaving more white candles in our wake.

I looked back and had to stop Bella too so we could look at the starry Milky Way that lay behind us and pushed us.

The woman with the vegetable cart halted next to us and called down. "Have an apple, have a pear!" She passed them down to us and Bella tied one of her flowers to the horse's mane.

As we walked along, everyone else had the same happiness too, as if every person in the crowd was someone we knew.

Bella pointed out the little electric truck as it weaved towards us and beeped its tinny horn. I almost didn't recognize the truck. It was covered with flapping strips of colored wallpaper.

"Hello!" yelled Peg. She slowed and leaned over to wave at us.

I grabbed her hand. "The war's over!" I laughed. I don't know how it happened but the war was over.

She gave me a mysterious smile, "Almost…" She grinned at me. "You'll see…" And with that, she waved farewell, steering back into the crowd, in a hurry to go somewhere.

60.

The untiring Saturn Circus wanted to leave nowhere in the city untouched by their presence. Over the bridge, they passed through downtown, where we stopped at last and sat on the marbled edge of a statue with running water.

I touched the smile on Bella's face. There was pale candlelight on her skin. She moved close into me. I whispered in her ear. She laughed sweetly and squeezed me. We listened to the spilling water.

It happened so unexpectedly we both jumped.

A bomb exploded and the sky shook like a great bird taking off. I held Bella tightly as I looked down the alley of gray buildings. A plume of smoke rose from a place not far away. I recognized the place.

"The Fortune Company!"

I could see its ripped apart roof. The explosion had thrown a cloud from inside. It blew quickly in the night wind, higher and higher. I covered Bella with my arms as the fallout passed overhead. The cloud over us rained down white debris into the street.

I opened my eyes. The breeze scattered the torn pulp everywhere. We were covered with thousands of bird nest strips. The feathery sound of the shower was paper with words.

I plucked a piece of the snow from Bella's hair and I read our fortune aloud. It was the end of every fairy tale.

ROME USED TO BE THE WORLD

In the days when the spinning wheels hummed busily...

—George Eliot

Part 1: Giant Food

Part 2: Super-8 Giant

Part 3: Into The Clouds

1.
GIANT FOOD

When Sherman Pond's day began, he had to reach far up the wall to get his card and punch the timeclock. 8:03 the numbers stamped. Oh dear, he worried, I'm late again. It's that rickety elevator that held me up. It clanks so slowly.

Above him, the rafters were slung with heavy spider webs and yellow buzzing lights that hung at crooked angles. At the far end, the window was paned into little dirty squares. In the feeble gray shine, the shapes of pigeons crowded outside on the ledge.

Sherman walked beside tables piled with bolts of cloth. The sewing machines whirred, tended by old women. Nobody held him for more than a glance as he passed.

In the corner of the room was a green metal table already peaked with work waiting for him. He fed his coat and hat to a hook on the wall behind him, then he climbed up the stool to be even with the table surface.

Tired already, he reached for the needle and the colored cloth to sew the white stars onto blue background. It was his part of making the flags that were sold and sent all over the world.

*****

At 5:03, finally, Sherman climbed off his stool and landed on the warped floor. The bin next to his table was full as a deep pool of water with blue squares. Pale stars swam around in it like fish.

He rubbed his hands together and cracked his sore knuckles. Every day lasted so long. He was so tired he just wanted to go home, eat and sleep.

Catching a yawn before it left his mouth, he stretched his arm up for his timecard. After so long at this job, he was used to where it should be, but the rack of employee cards felt strange to him. It was lower…lower by a couple of inches. It confused his senses.

Funny…He bit his lip…Another joke on Short Sherman…Someone at the shop always had a gag for him. But as he punched the clock with his timecard, again his arm didn't have to lift so high.

He sighed, "They've been extra clever today."

The shop, hissing like an empty seashell, ticked his footsteps crossing to the door. Then, when he reached for the worn brass colored door knob, Sherman stopped again. It was different too. It was also lower.

The whole office had been prepared, and the elevator handle, and the worn buttons inside, and the door to the street, and on and on…

All the way home, he kept experiencing the change, as if the entire world had got a little smaller.

He felt dizzy and sick by the time he stood before his apartment door. There was another notice on it, written in the manager's frantic, threatening handwriting. Sherman put it in his pocket with the others and left the hallway.

It took him all day to get back home.

In a moment, he faced his square carved room, set with a pair of windows, a kitchen and the opened door leading to a bedroom. Shadows striped the walls like a canary cage.

The phonograph was playing a scratchy record, as old as street pavement. She was in the kitchen with her blue curved back to him, boiling water and cutting vegetables. Carrots and cabbages splashed into the pot. At the sound of his creak, she looked over her shoulder.

"Ethyll," he sighed, "I don't feel too good."

He sat down in the rocking chair next to the phonograph. The arm rests pinched into his sides. "Something's wrong..." His shirt cuffs were up past his wrists, he loosened his strangling tie and breathed deeply.

Ethyll left the kitchen and came over to stand near. Everyday work wore him out. She was used to it.

He looked into her face desperately, "Am I dreaming or what?" The chair squeezed him like a wooden python. "I can't—" he twisted anxiously and stood up suddenly.

"Look!" he said loudly, "Can't you tell I'm different?"

An awkward silence sawed.

He put his hands softly to her hips, but they didn't feel like they used to. She held herself the way a tree does. She gave him such a tired look it hurt to watch.

"You can see it too," he said and let her go. They couldn't even hold each other the same way. If it wasn't for the record and the boiling water,

the room would be empty. If only there was something he could do to make her happy. There was
too much sadness here, loss and need, failure and
hopelessness, there was nothing he could do...Or
only one thing. Yes...With the end of the song
crackling away next to him, Sherman turned and
left for the door. She didn't say anything, so he
kept going.

*****

As he walked along the crowded sidewalk, he could feel himself continue to grow, stretching through his clothes. The concrete echoed and every block a button would pop. It wasn't going to stop. He stared around anxiously for somewhere to hide, somewhere dark.

Before the seams of his suit ripped all the way open, he stopped at a theater window and fished a dollar from his tight pocket.

"Let me have a ticket," he told the girl behind the glass.

"The picture started a half hour ago," she replied.

"I don't care!"

He paid and grabbed the ticket from her and rushed through the doors. In the red carpet lobby he ran past the big posters of Boris Karloff, the popcorn machines and plaster columns, towards the sounds of a monster behind the velvet drapes.

It was black in the aisle. By the silver and gray shine on the screen, he could see a small audience watching the film. Pulling off his tight shoes, leaving them on the dark carpet, he hid himself in the back row under the river glow of movie light. What else could he do?

*****

A bright fire ended the monster's reign. Credits moved. After a flickering pause for the switch of rolls, the second feature quickly began.

If only I could stop this growing, Sherman worried...I have to concentrate all I can on the film and maybe I will...Still, he couldn't deny the tearing electricity feeling, nor could he keep his clothing from ripping off in mummy shrouds. By the time Boris Karloff was again endangering the world, the last of old Sherman Pond had been shed to the floor and pushed under the chairs.

Nobody seemed to notice that more than a screen monster was in the seats behind them. The movie played on while he grew.

He stretched over twelve chairs, lying down, the illuminated Giant who tried his best to stay a part of the shadows.

The orchestral music and a woman screaming in fear shook from the wall speakers, as the creature was felled in the last struggle before the credits.

The Giant burrowed into the gap between the chairs. It wasn't a good time for monsters.

He pressed across the sticky floor to shade himself from the returning houselights.

*****

Minutes of footsteps and waiting tensed and prickled his skin. Luckily none of the people drifting out or entering, looking for seats close to the screen, noticed the jammed dark long shape in the back row.

If only the movies would hurry and start again, the Giant worried. Maybe I will begin to return to normal size. This can't go on forever, he hoped. There has to be a limit for me.

The Giant sighed as the theater hushed. The lights dimmed to repeat the double feature again. He needed to get out of his cramped position. Awkwardly, he pushed himself up.

For a moment his shoulder blurred across the corner of the screen, a shadow on the film, then he quickly pressed his back to the wall, put his legs over the chairs to face the screen hunched under the projector stream.

It worked for a while, but he was still growing fast, so quickly that however he twisted he couldn't avoid casting a silhouette on the screen. That couldn't go unnoticed too long in a theater so small.

He watched two people below him look up at the ceiling. A couple seconds might have passed before they screamed. From then on, it didn't take long for the entire room to whirl with panic and everyone was shouting and scrambling for the green exit lights.

Straddling overhead with the spiders, the Giant watched them scatter. Most of the movie was playing on his reflecting skin or dripping off in pieces onto the screen. Moving like a cloud towards the vision of haunted Boris Karloff, the Giant stopped and crouched in the front row.

With a sudden flail he tore the gold curtains down. Wrapping the two halves around himself, tucking the ends into folds, he resembled a Pharaoh towering over the chairs.

He felt like screaming too, but what could he do?

The projectionist had run out with the crowd leaving the movie playing. The Giant stood in the middle of it, lifted his arms, pressed them against the screen and with a push, he broke through the wall.

*****

Bricks fell across the sidewalk in a cloud of smoke. The Giant looked in all directions.

There were cars slowing and crashing into each other. People looked child sized.

The movie still played rays around him, through the crashed theater wall, landing on a tenement building across the street. People ran from him to hide around corners, to watch from far away.

He was fifty feet tall and the bright theater curtains shined all the light bulbs and neon tubes of the city. He could have been a fireworks display.

Swayed for a moment, he was jumpy as a tornado churned on the avenue. In thundering strides, he weaved his way past the stalled traffic.

*****

Sylas Warner should have known better. His room was hung with strips of film hanging from the ceiling. He went back and forth between them, talking to himself, finding a strip and bringing it to the splicer, to add another scene to the movie he was making.

"Rents paid..." he mumbled, "I can get a job next week..." He tied one moment to another. "I got seven days to work on this, nonstop. No worries or interruptions, God willing. Knock on wood," he added, knuckling the slanted desk.

Police sirens screamed past his barred window. He wasn't distracted. It was just another noise, like the buzzing of flies in his kitchen. A couple more went by then he wondered, "Must be a robbery...maybe a shootout." Another siren howled.

Sylas returned to his work. He fed the images of a monster into the editor. A pretty girl in the frames remained unaware and innocent, as the monster crept up on her.

"Here he comes..." Sylas said, "Out of the shadows." He cut where the monster began to reach for her. "Next shot."

The floorboards of his room shook as a subway train shot through the dark tunnel underneath the floor. "A Brooklyn worm..." he imagined and he paused, inspired, "Remember this idea... There are huge radioactive worms living under New York... Okay... They dig into the subway canals and eat the people on the trains. Great!! *The Brooklyn Worms*...Brilliant!"

He went happily back to work, pulling down another line of celluloid. "I have to remember that." He squinted at the little picture of film.

The floor continued to shake, even after the train was gone. In fact the tremors were growing stronger. His work table rocked on its spindly legs. "What is this?!"

It was like one of his films or nightmares.

The shaking and pausing approach could have been the footsteps of an atomic freak thirty stories tall.

Sylas moved over to the cracked window and stared out the bars. The angle showed the dilapidated buildings across the street, crumbling and holding desperately to the night clouds to keep from falling down.

The sky was shot with searchlights. They webbed over the impossibly tall man who walked along the skyline. It was as beautiful as a perfect special effect.

In just a few steps the Giant was gone, the vibrations of his gate ebbed, and all Sylas could do was stand there in wonder with a clip of film.

*****

On a hill in a house overlooking the bowl of city lights, the footsteps couldn't put a dent in the chirping crickets violining the moon. A window was open so the wind could blow through the room.

In that slight push, the puppets and green ivy plants turned over her bed. That sound made her stir. She was leaving some dream.

Her blue eyes clicked camera like. The room was alive with shadows catapulted onto the walls from the little blue nightlight. There were animal toys on the shelves to protect her. The floor slightly shook. Something was in the air. A storm, she decided and turned in the knitted blankets to fall back asleep.

*****

The Giant found a place that was quiet, in an alley made of tall warehouses on either side with a brick wall at his back. The river waves splashed the pier stilted legs. Close to his ears, the pigeons in the eaves rustled and cooed. Stars tried to spy through the gray and silver clouds that pooled in sky. He found he could finally calm down.

Here I am…I've been lucky…I escaped. But he didn't know if he would stop growing.

He rested in the stillness. He sat down and put his face against his knees.

All the changing made him so tired. In the moonlight, a long narrow ship sparkled the water. The Giant could hear it for a long time. Its motor chopped like a little wind-up toy.

*****

The papers, the radios and the early morning television screens glared with the crazy news of the Giant. Is he dangerous? Everyone wanted to know. The military was ready in case they were needed. The roads of the city crowded with cars.

People watched the skyline as they started for work. There were towers and clouds, trees and birds, but nobody saw a hundred foot man.

Traffic and crowds wobbled at the block with the big marquee and its spilled bricks. Police still swarmed around the broken movie theater, making chalk marks and yellow tape. Detectives poured across the remains.

A crowd of people were gathered there. Reporters from newspapers groomed through the noise. And a woman in a long black dress and shawl stood drawn like a fairytale widow. She watched from the roped off corner. Ethyll knew what happened. She hadn't been able to sleep, thinking about it. It was Sherman. She knew. She stared regretfully at the movie theater, wrapped her arms tighter under the black shawl and she watched all the people digging over what he left behind. They could try all day to figure it out and they would never know what happened. "He's gone," she whispered to no one.

*****

The sun tacked a yellow carpet yard by yard down the alleyway. The day rumbled in the harbor. The Giant woke up. Just stretching, his elbow knocked a hole in the warehouse wall.

"Sorry," he muttered. Bricks rubbed into piles.

He could see in the warehouse wall. The green fluorescent lights revealed rows of stacked food. Reaching in, his massive hand took a pallet of wrapped bread loaves. He couldn't help it, he was so hungry.

His body responded by growing another ten feet.

A cloud of pigeons took to the air.

Strong and tall as he was, he knew he better be careful. He needed somewhere safer to hide, while he tried to decide what was happening to him. He crouched and took a look over the roof.

The city spread for miles. He wobbled like one of those sunflowers that bends its yellow, too heavy face.

The river, he quickly decided, before I'm seen…

In one quick step, he reached the end of the pier. I can live in the river, hide under the waves, who would know I'm there?

The water rose over his knees. Quickly, he submerged himself, staying close to the shadows under the docks so every now and then he could surface and breathe.

*****

At the three o'clock bell, she ran from the school. A streamer of stars flew back from her hand and she sang out the gate in the fenced playground, across the street, running all the way to the corner. Cars stopped to wait. There was a strange charged feeling in the air—all anyone could do was watch the horizon for a sign of the monster the radio couldn't stop warning about. She ran to the other side where the green park began. Climbing a tree was a good place to start. She was going Giant hunting.

*****

The world shimmered like a stainglass window image. Boats trailing wakes, sun glow and slicks of clouds above. The Giant's back lay in the soft mud of the river bed. The daylight floated in the current, fish slept in his hair.

The more he lay there, the more he thought of the things he could do. I may not be this way forever, he kept reminding himself, why not make some changes. He thought about the factory and all the things that had made life so hard. Now I could topple them like cards! Everywhere I wanted to, I could make life better for everyone. I could scoop open the banks and throw the money around like rain—wouldn't everyone think I was a miracle?

I can do anything I want...

When he sat up, the river ran off down his shoulders. He bumped his head on the pier ceiling. A seagull flew away screaming. It was early evening. Hesitating by the slump of an old docked barge, he waited for the sky to get a little darker, a little safer for a Giant to walk about.

*****

After a whole day of begging around, in and out of doors, pawnshops, hotel rooms, pool halls, street corners, Sylas was able to get some dollars together. Talking to himself, bursting into song at the thought, he hurried across the avenue.

His image grew in the storefront window.

The Shutterbug was Open 9-4. A blinking neon sign of a bee held a camera.

Sylas opened the door and went in like a Hollywood star-maker. "Voyle!" he called boisterously to the counter. "I need film!"

A tired looking old man lowered a newspaper from in front of his bleary eyes. With infinite patience, he groaned and puffed on the cigar stub jammed in his mouth.

Sylas stopped at the counter. "I want four rolls of Super-8." Fishing in his pocket, he spread change across the smoky glass counter. He ordered the quarters and dimes and nickels in checker shapes. "You heard about the Giant, Voyle?"

The old man still regarded him sadly and silently, wallpapery.

Sylas grinned and slapped the counter, "He's my new movie star."

*****

"Goodnight," the girl yawned.

Lying in her warm bed, she listened to her parents whisper and leave, fading footsteps into their room down the hall, then she rolled to the edge of her blankets waterfall.

She reached down to pull a paper grocery bag onto the covers in front of her. A warm cricket wind blew the curtains and spun the hanging plants.

After all day hoping, searching the park after school, looking in the back-lots and tunnels fed by railroad tracks, it was night but not time to give up. She took some candies from the bag, enough to fill a hill on her palm, and she turned around to line them on the paint chipped windowsill.

"Mr. Giant," she said, "here's some food for you."

She leaned with her chin on the wood to look at the trees, the little glowing clover fields patched around the slopes, the moon in the clouds.

"So..." she could see the grassy yard, "If you want to, you can sleep down there." She pictured him, his mossy long body asleep. She brightened, "In the morning we could go to school together." Like a story book...For as long as she could stay awake, she listened for the footsteps that would be him.

*****

Despite all his plans for his brand new height, the Giant kept haunting himself with a memory. Back at their apartment, Ethyll would be awake in bed and probably crying and try as he might he couldn't forget.

It's no use. I'll never be more than Sherman Pond.

Getting out of his hiding place displaced the river onto the cement coat of land. He walked in long powerful strides even though he knew, Soon I'll be where everyone can see me. I'll stand at the height of their buildings, caught in spotlights, and I'll only hope that—his thoughts stopped as a car swerved around his ankle. The toy-like Pontiac scurried past him. When it disappeared, he kept setting his gigantic feet upon the street. He wondered if he should sing or whistle or hum to let them know he was coming...

Across the jagged line of staggering building shapes the Giant moved. His steps meshed with the sleepy rundown sounds of the waterfront, the train trestles, the trams, buses and indoor noises of those getting ready for bed.

He could see a certain tired home, distant, tipped between the city lights.

*****

230

Sylas had been waiting.

The moment he felt the floor begin to shake, he was ready. On the way out the door, he grabbed his camera, stuffed the film cartons into the shaggy pockets of his overcoat and he ran to his car.

Parked next to the fire hydrant, the windshield wipers held down a full deck of traffic tickets.

The night flared and the Giant's silhouette scraped over the roofs, screeches and nervous howling.

"I knew you'd be back!" Sylas bleated, trying to start the car.

It coughed.

"Come on!" He kangarooed the gas pedal, "Let's go!"

A rusty blue cloud coughed out of the exhaust pipe. The motor quilted uncertainly but he put the car into motion quickly.

The slab of Detroit metal rolled from a sickly cloud onto the street, noisily gathering speed, through a red light, as he steered towards the halo of searchlights blocks away.

*****

Ethyll had a book open on her lap. Kitchen light shined across the page. The record needle swished in the groove at the vinyl's end. Her head was dipped, she was asleep.

At the intervals of a slow beating heart, the window glass rattled. Moaning sirens approached. A sweep of searchlights pawed the ashy sky.

The wooden floor swayed more and more.

All through the apartment building the muffled noises changed into a panicky scratch.

The book slid off Ethyll's leg. Her tired, swollen eyes startled open.

The room shook again.

Dried flowers fell from the mantelpiece and cracks formed on the walls.

Just as she got to her feet, the earthquake stopped.

There were screams, the electricity blinked off and on, police car sirens, as a shaft of bright spotlight hit through the window and turned everything x-ray white.

Suddenly it was eclipsed. The room became shadow. A voice filled the space as if was just for the abalone curl of her ear alone.

He tried to hush the sound of his gigantic words, but they were like wind. "Ethyll, are you there?" He looked into the purple and blue. "Ethyll?"

A little twig doll moved to the window. The glass pushed open and there she was.

"Ethyll..." He could barely discern her. He had lost the sight of her features. "Ethyll, don't be afraid," he said as her hands went to her tiny face.

"I'm—" he knew he couldn't try to touch her or hold her, "I'll try to make things better..."

and he couldn't help it, for a second he started to
cry. Swimming pools fell from his eyes, crashing
on the cement and cars.

Ethyll reached at the swerve of him leaving.
Saying his name didn't even carry to him.

In such wide steps hurry, he led the police
and lights and crazy sounds, steepling off towards
the river again.

*****

When Sylas' car ran over a nail on the railroad tracks, the steering wheel jerked and shuddered in his grip, followed by the flop-flop-flopping of the uneven tire.

Garbage cans fell out of his way as he stopped. "No!"

So close to his camera, out of range, the Giant shambled on to disappear in roofs.

*****

That night the river overflowed.

Hundreds of people lined the banks to pile sandbags to hold it back. The warm stormy current poured across the streets, taking over land.

Under the waves was the Giant, underneath the circling boats. Seagulls windmilled in flocks over the spot where the bubbles formed.

By dawn the pools went for blocks towards downtown. The boats were tucked back into shore. It took the day and the sun and machines pumping water for the river to flow back to normal.

Later on, life resumed. A barge took a cargo towards the sea, ferries tipped from shore to shore. Everything could have been the same old photograph.

Another hour passed.

From a small dock upstream, a black boat pulled out cautiously. It swerved in the current to a drifting halt and a man leaned over the side.

The man stared through his reflection into the deep green, then he fished a microphone cord down into the wet.

"Hello, Giant," the voice on the ship called from it.

Covered in Dracula-colored weeds, the Giant listened. He wiped his eyes.

"Giant, can you hear me? If you're still there, please appear."

The boat tossed uncertainly.

The drifting microphone repeated, "Hello, Giant." The two words eeled. More followed, "I have an offer for you...Can you hear me? Please appear."

The Giant needed to breathe anyway. He

could use some food too. Sitting up brought his head close enough to the surface to be in bluish rays. Folds of water disturbed with him.

"Hello, Giant..."

When his head burst out, he exhaled the stale gale kept in his lungs for so long, across the harbor front. Tin roofs flapped wings, a row of sandbags flew into air, parked cars slid, things smashed and crumpled in the wind.

The Giant unsealed his eyes. A froth of water encircled him. Close by, a bathtub paddle boat went up and down. While he breathed in and out, he let the river calm.

Riding high waves, the boat was pushing to get closer. It sailed up to the giant's chest where the bow chopped the water there. Like an amplified beetle it spoke, "Hello, Giant."

He watched it wheel in closer.

"I have a proposition for you...You may have heard of the Saturn Circus..." The tiny man in the bow waved the microphone, "We'd like you to join us."

The Giant shifted and sent a ripple that shook the boat.

The circus man continued urgently, "We won't ask much of you. You'll be rich."

The Giant reached his arm out to cup the water around the boat. Then he lifted the handful up to his face. "I don't need money anymore," he thundered. He wanted to throw the boat ten miles, then he remembered his old life and the pain still there and he reconsidered. "But I know someone who does...I will work for you if you pay her."

*****

236

Sweeping lights ran fingers across the folds of tent stretched high over the field. An orchestra played for the crowds filling pine bleachers. Stars broke through clouds, the band struck a fanfare, and the ringmaster glided in from the stalks and wildflowers to stop in spotlight.

"Ladies and gentlemen...The Saturn Circus is proud to present the world's latest wonder!"

Underneath the sewn together tents, the tallest man listened to the introduction and music with his eyes shut. This will make you happy Ethyll, he thought. I will change the world for you. After tonight, you will never be poor. Whatever you need can be yours. He pictured her smiling. That fantasy kept him going.

The sky began to reveal, as the sheets of canvas fell away, the stars, the treads of glossy clouds and there in the middle of the opened tent, taking up half the universe, was the Giant. In his hands he held elephants.

*****

Each night the Saturn Circus lit up the horizon, the girl would watch from her window. Far across the leaves and hills, the glow shifted on the black curve of land whenever the spotlights swung. Her white blanket wrapped warmly over her shoulders.

Watching the distance, she held her arms out. She wished she could turn them into wings. "I could fly over there and land on his hand."

The walls of her room were taped with crayoned drawings and faint newspaper photos of the Giant. He balanced juggling acts, held a loco-motive train, lifted a lion tamer and all of his cats.

She flapped her soft covered wings, but she didn't rise. She sighed and lowered her arms, "Oh well." There was always the chance that he would arrive for the giant food left on her windowsill.

*****

2.
SUPER-8 GIANT

Summer's end blew in off the sea, up the miles of river to the city. The leaves rubbed together in the gathering breeze, loosening. Crows circled brown and green trees. The softer flowers wagged off their last bright petals. The rest would wake up cold in dew. Everywhere the warmer season could be felt leaving, retreating the streets and neighborhoods, going back to find the sun.

In the field outside the limits of town, the circus fairgrounds were tearing down. Steel towers let go of tents, unroped. All the animals found their homes in cages again, the painted caravan doors opened and closed and costumes were put away.

The Giant, the circus star, sat brooding like a jagged mountain peak in fallow brown weeds. What will I do now? Where will I go? His breathing rumbled, so deep in thought, it was a long time before he noticed the black and white dress waving and waving to him.

The woman, no bigger than an inch, called his real long-lost name, "Sherman...Sherman..." like a rustle of ladybug wings.

"Ethyll," the sky answered, "I wanted you to come see me. Where have you been?" He lay down so he could hear her. The circus master had given him a golden, trumpet-shaped cone so he could hear what people said. He pointed it from his ear to her.

Still, she had to scream into the air. "I tried to be with you. I couldn't...I kept thinking of you all the time."

He tried to think of something to say to her. They were so far from each other. "Did you get the circus money?" He couldn't hear her reply. He said, "They said they were sending you all the money I earned." He put the horn over her.

Her words were only raindrops, "No," she said. "I don't know what you mean."

"They promised me you'd be a millionaire. The only reason I've been working this circus is for you."

"I don't have any money."

It sunk in. He rose into a storm from her little flower size. "Wait here, Ethyll. Don't leave."

Three steps were all it took to stand beside the rust and silver trailer. Grabbing it, he pulled it into air and peeled the roof off like a sardine can.

The little ringmaster was pressed against the wall inside, squeaking, holding his arms in front of himself.

"You lied to me," the Giant's voice rumbled. He was so compelled to do something terrible.

"Give me the money you owe."

The Giant eyes glared down.

The tiny man staggered over the angled floor, wrenched open a safe dug into the tin wall. He took out a bag and offered it. He let it go on the Giant's fingertip.

The air became ground again, the tiny man slumped pale against the floor, bent to a cruel angle.

Three steps away, the Giant found Ethyll, still waiting for him. He kneeled and opened his palm so she could step on. "Let me take you home," he said.

*****

"What happened to your movie?" Voyle asked.

Sylas was taken by surprise. He was seizing a bag of rice so tightly it almost exploded. "Voyle!" he cried.

"I haven't seen your face at my shop for a long time. How's your Giant movie?"

"My movie..." groaned Sylas, spinning, "That circus took my star. I can't film him when he's juggling elephants, it's demeaning." In truth, he thought, I can't afford a ticket...This rice is even pushing the budget, there's only change in my pocket... "It was better when he was walking around the city."

"That's too bad," Voyle said.

"Momentary bad luck," Sylas explained, "But somehow I'll get to him. I've got a good idea for a movie that will change the world."

Voyle studied him for a moment longer. "Okay, well good luck." He began to push his grocery cart again.

Sylas was almost drooling at the mountain of food stacked in Voyle's cart. "Ummm..." he hooked a finger in the metal side of it reluctantly, "Say Voyle...You don't have any spare change do you?"

A look of pained unsurprise crossed Voyle's face. He dug into his pocket for his wallet.

*****

Ethyll climbed carefully off his hand, onto the fire-escape outside her window. She was dizzy and practically falling down, but she tried to stay strong as long as he stayed near.

He set the money onto the grate at her feet. "This is what they paid me for carrying elephants, picking up carrousels and spinning trolley cars... all those circus things they made me do. I went through it for you because I want you to be happy. We never had a chance like this. Now you can wish any wish and it will come true."

Cars were jamming the avenue at his feet. It amazed him how quickly the city would find him and cloud around him.

He was relieved that he couldn't hear her through the noise. Putting his hand out, he reached for her, though he couldn't tell for sure. "Good-bye," he whispered, leaving her with what he could never give while he was Sherman Pond. Now that was done, he could take himself somewhere else, where he could try to forget.

******

This time the Giant went by in the night, Sylas was out of his apartment in a second. His shoes slipped and echoed. Three cats leaped off the dark hood and roof of his car as he pulled the door open.

The car started like an old factory. The worn engine parts curdled, turned, coughed blue exhaust out the tailpipe. "You're not getting away this time!"

To keep the Giant in sight, he had to weave cross streets and alleys in his shuddering car. The Giant's shoulders glowed in the yellow city lights, way up into purple clouds.

"Come on! Make way!" Sylas flicked his hand off the wheel, "Get out of my way!" The wake of the striding Giant churned with people pouring out to stare.

Waving his arm from the window, Sylas cried, "I'm a filmmaker! Let me through!"

With the crowd ebbing across the street, bicycles too and barking dogs, children singing and chasing games, the whole thing was changing into a kind of holiday. Sylas had to slow the car into a painful halt. The street was jammed. He buried his face in his arms, drained on the wheel as the warped hood gave a dry sigh and began to steam hopelessly.

*****

Under night's moon, the girl left the house she'd been wishing in. "I can hear you, leaves," she told the familiar trees, the willows, the oaks and maples, the elm that spread many arms.

On her back was a blue pack filled with just the things she couldn't leave behind. She carried a mockingbird toy, a battery powered flower, a blanket and tarp, clothes and a book by Dr. Seuss.

The weeds swished past her legs. The hill fell steeply into a valley where she met a paved road. Her singing carried her along.

*****

Ethyll returned to the Saturn Circus, to a black tin trailer on the edge of town, to a door painted with gold and silver stars. Inside, in the red amber light of the small metal room, she asked, "Can you help me?"

There was a shuffling. A crystal ball winked with trapped fireflies.

Ethyll took out a handful of money from under her long coat and offered it. "I need magic to get back to him."

The crystal ball drew her closer.

*****

After the Giant sunk in the river again, he swam like a salmon heading upstream, scratching along the bed of it. There was broken machinery, sunken junk, sand amid the natural curves of the course. Had a whale ever gone as far upstream? Never. Yet there he went, urging himself to continue.

Past overgrown embankments where factories poured their metal leftovers, into slow moving eddies where pretty green lily pads pet the surface in places, and on to where farms spilled off the chemicals they grew. He and the swirling water washed it all away.

Every half hour, he broke the current to breathe. Air restored what it was to be alive. He breathed deeply and went under again. He was careful making sure no one knew he was there.

*****

The girl followed the riverbank, on a dirt path near the railroad track. Flowed in the leaves, she could watch the water for signs of the Giant.

Running away from home, with every step she got further away. "I have to see the Giant. I'll catch up with him as soon as he gets out of the river. I'll just keep going too."

To keep her from feeling alone, she thought of *The Wind In The Willows*. Mr. Mole and his friend Rat were rowing in the lilies close by, keeping her company.

She became so used to the forest and tumbling river sounds that she could hear the car a mile before it appeared. Actually, it made enough noise to be a mechanical dinosaur.

She was lying in the ferns, watching from a hiding place, when it appeared.

It was hard to tell it was a car. It was a rusted disaster crumpled down upon flopping squared tires. Getting slower and slower, at last it gave up in front of her.

The engine rasped and fainted. The world was left to its wind again.

The girl stayed frozen low to the ground and watched the door groan open.

A man got out. He wore a shabby collection of clothes. He was so upset he kicked the tire. After that shock he hopped up and down on one leg, holding his shoe.

When he got calmer, he hobbled to the silvery grill and opened the hood.

A genie of steam unfurled.

He's one of those poor men who talk to themselves, she observed. She had seen them before in the city. He stood beside the broken car and didn't seem to know what to do.

That's when she surprised herself by standing and walking towards him. He didn't even register her until she was there, looking into the burnt colored brown engine parts.

"Where are you going?" she asked.

He jumped.

"If you want to start a car," she told him, "you have to say the right words. This is what I would say..."

Sylas listened to the girl talk to his car. He couldn't believe the way she had appeared out of this nowhere, to try working a spell.

"You can start it now," she told him.

Such a little child, but she was so sure, she had convinced him.

He got back behind the wheel and turned the key, pressed the gas pedal and sure enough the car came to life.

The hood fell closed with a slam and there she stood in front, hazeled like an angel mechanic.

Sylas leaned out his window and tried to treat the miracle casually, "Thank you very much." But when she stepped out of the way and he tried to go forward, the car couldn't leave her shadow. The engine stopped.

The girl walked over and put her hands on the hood and that simply restarted it.

"I think..." Sylas said in a slow realization, "You have power over my car. If you don't come along with me, I'll end up walking. Are you going that way?" He pointed down the forest road in front of them.

"I'm searching for the Giant," she said.

"Me too! I'm making a movie with him."

"You are?" She got close, "Do you know him?"

"I've got four rolls of film. All I need to do is find him. It's going to be a masterpiece."

"Well, I'll come with you. It will be faster by car." She hurried to the other side and got inside. She crinkled her nose at the interior, the sharp smell of rainy metal chalk.

"The car likes you," he said. "It's never driven so well, it sounds brand new." The car kicked aside the fallen yellow leaves with a roar.

"I'm Caroline," she introduced herself. "What's your name, Mister?"

"I'm Sylas Warner. I make movies."

"Like what?"

"You might have seen some of them. There's a chance. They were mostly low budget...*Carefree Carnival, The Ostrich, Two Gallows*...Oh, I've made so many I can't remember. They're floating around the circuit, I guess. I don't even know where most of them have ended up. There's so many."

"The only movies I've seen are the ones in school, or if I can't sleep, sometimes I watch the late night movie on TV. I saw a scary Dracula."

Sylas took his eyes off the road in excitement, "Was the movie in black and white with a castle? Did Dracula have a strange way of talking? Did he creep and turn into a bat? Was there lots of fog, close-ups on his hypnotizing shiny stare?"

"Most of the time I closed my eyes. I was watching it alone."

"Oh, you should never be alone," Sylas said, "You have to watch movies with someone. Especially that old Dracula movie. It's my favorite. Everything I do is a reflection." He shook his head in respect. The deep forest glided past in the windows. "You have to have something that inspires you, to carry with you forever."

He pointed out the windshield at all the green, "This could be a movie too—the movie of our search for the Giant."

*****

251

As the sun dropped lower and the moon was raised up the mast of a tree to float in the sky, Sylas stopped the car. They were in a clearing.

"We'll find some wood for a fire," he said, "and we can sleep for the night."

With the light they had left, they scoured the ground among the fallen logs and ferns, picking up big armfuls of twigs and branches. Some newspaper helped get the fire going.

"Do you think we'll see the Giant tomorrow?" said Caroline. She held her hands out to the warmth.

"We must be getting near. He might even be out there right now," where the dark river clattered, "sleeping on the rock bed with salmon swimming around." Sylas paused to try and catch sight of him. "I wonder why he stays in the river."

Caroline put a birch's white hem on the flame. "I think he's lonely. Thinking he's the only one in the world makes him sad." She listened hard to the water talking over the stones. "I hope we see him soon." She unrolled her tarp and blanket and lay down.

They watched the fire dance its bright leaves.

Until Sylas said, "Goodnight Caroline," and went to go sleep on his car seat, leaving the door open and colored by the glow.

She yawned. The wood turned into black and white feathers as the fire started to fall asleep with her.

The stream was the only sound in the world.

*****

Bells were ringing in the water and a flute played as mournful as a sad woman sighing somewhere deep in the river.

The sound woke Caroline up.

She looked at the blackness around her. Above her the stars hung ornaments in the trees. Water rushed along noisily, making a million different songs, and the more she listened, the more she heard voices too. She couldn't tell if it was magic or not.

The bells and flute grew louder. They seemed to rise out of the very middle of the swirling river flow.

"Something is happening," she whispered. She didn't want to wake Sylas, though she could hear him tossing with some bad dream.

She pulled the blanket tighter. By the time sleep took her away again, the whole river was playing the sad lullaby.

*****

In the morning, Caroline woke up in a cold curled shape. The fire was crackling again. Sylas was kneeling, feeding it. She stretched and rubbed her arms.

"Good morning," Sylas smiled.

She yawned and waved.

"Did you sleep okay?"

Looking at the river, everything appeared to have settled into a painting again. The scene made her wonder if anything had really gone on. She couldn't tell.

"I had the most bizarre dreams," Sylas said. "On and on, they were like movies, stranger than belief." He stirred the fire around with a branch. The smoke shifted.

He cleared his throat, stood up with an empty pan, "Once I make some coffee we can start the Giant search."

"Can I get the water for you?" Caroline asked, jumping to her feet and climbing out into daylight.

She took the pan from him and hopped over the patches of sunlight, to the edge of land. Stones and driftwood gave her dry steps out into the river.

A pool of clear mountain water slowly turned. By sitting on the big black rock she could dip the pan in.

Something rippling through the water caught her eyes. It glinted as she leaned forward.

Pebbles covered all but the gold corner.

The pool was as deep as her arm and icy cold.

Past her elbow, she reached for and touched the treasure. A cloud of sand and gravel spilled off, murking the pool as she pulled the thing into air.

It was a small gold picture frame with glass covering the photograph inside. A beautiful sad-eyed Cinderella in black and white, her dark hair was tied with violets and leaves, her black dress from the old days trimmed in lace.

"Someone must have dropped you in the river a hundred years ago," Caroline said. She shook it dry and hid it in a pocket.

Scooping water to mix coffee in, she balanced on the mossy steps leading back to the woods.

*****

They drove for less than a half hour before the road ended in more holes and branches than pathway. The car lurched into a growth of young pines.

Sylas turned helplessly to Caroline. "I think this is as far as we can go."

He opened his door and pushed against the ferns. The engine turned off. The forest filled their ears with wind in tall firs.

Not far away the river breathed. Beyond, it seemed like something else that could move was holding still.

Caroline got out and slung on her backpack. The green went on and on.

Sylas was going through the things in the backseat, finding the film equipment he needed. He had a bag he put them in.

"Okay," he stood back up, closed the door. He put his hands on the mottled primered rooftop, "Car, stay here. Take care. Don't leave, we'll be back in a while."

*****

Along the silver channel wash there were signs that he had traveled there. A branch held a ripped shred of gold curtain cloth.

Sylas and Caroline stopped next to another clue.

Forming a shallow, a footprint was left close to the shore. It held fingerling salmon clowning around. The footprint showed travel out of the river.

"He's walking now." Sylas looked up at the skyline of green trees. "Maybe he's hiding out there in the forest...They're so tall he could sit in them and who would know."

Caroline bounced over the rocks, away from the water footprint.

Sylas saw her wave from a ragged clearcut.

Not so far away, she sang, "Here's another one!" She stopped, almost falling in.

Sylas looked beyond her. A pair of ravens scratched out of the trees, cawing, revealing the broken Giant path that crooked through the forest. Branches hung in snaps. "Caroline!" he called.

By then she noticed it too. The ground in front of her flowered, crowded with dandelions. They grew in a winding yellow flow off into the dark green. She ran around the big footprint to go discover where they went.

Sylas had to hurry to keep track of the girl. She flickered in the shade and light. When he stopped to catch his breath, he marveled, "Look at all these daisies...I have to get my camera."

3.
INTO THE CLOUDS

No stranger than anything else she had seen, the flowers among her got taller and taller. The floppy yellow petals brushed her and covered her clothes with gold pollen. In the darkness of the woods the dandelions beamed like lanterns, opened up like paperback books. She pushed them aside, going further.

*****

Every once in a while Sylas would stop to film another scene. The huge flowers swayed in the frame. "Where am I?" he wondered.

*****

Caroline sat down to rest with her back against a maple-sized dandelion. More grew in trees everywhere, spreading yellow umbrellas overhead. A little wind made the tattered edges rattle.

She remembered the photo she found and she took it from her pocket. The pretty fairytale princess of sadness looked at her. The black and white of her shined out from the gold frame. She was almost too much for Caroline to look at; someone from the dreamworld.

The woman's eyes were water, the lips of the lady were parting and words promised, "Keep going and you will find him."

Caroline was so surprised that she trapped the princess back into her sweater pocket.

Noisily, all the tall flowers weaved to-and-fro.

*****

"Caroline!" Sylas held his Super-8 camera to his chest.

Underneath a dandelion ten feet tall, he listened to the sleepy reply of breeze and creaking flowers.

"Caroline!" he called.

*****

Just a few steps away from a fallen tree, Caroline stopped. The tree lay so oddly upon the moss and earth, as if its brown wooden curves and length was actually the shape of a person instead. White flowers grew around it. Sunlight filtered down in steam.

"Hello?" Caroline said. "How do you do?" Her skin prickled and she looked at her hand. A ladybug burred a red circle. She looked up and caught her breath.

The tree was a woman. She was sitting now, watching Caroline. She wore a green soft dress net made of moss and her hair fell maple and oak leaves over her shoulders. "Can you help me out of the ground?" her tree voice purred.

Caroline walked over, keeping her eyes in the tree-woman's green gaze. She reached her hand to the cedar fingers held out to her. The bark hand she touched was rough, but warm. They clasped. Their grip tightened.

The tree -woman said, "If you and I pull together, I can be free." Her brown legs tapered into the forest floor where her feet were trapped underground.

"I'll try," said Caroline and she took a stance.

As they pulled, the ground rippled, slow to let go. The ferns and plants around danced. Then one last draw together and the tree-woman's bare feet were out.

She laughed. She was so unsteadily uprooted, "Oh! I've never walked before." She took a step and swayed her body. "All my life I leaned against the wind. I could only imagine how it must feel to be free." She took a deep breath and she swelled her chest, shook her leafy hair and laughed.

Walking and wobbling happily, she almost sang, "I've watched the animals for so long, memorizing how to walk..." Keeping a hand on Caroline, she took another unrhymed step, "But it's harder than I thought it would be." She stopped and held on to the girl. Even though she was resting, her body wanted to keep going. "It's so beautiful to move."

"I've been walking for days," Caroline told her.

"Yes," said the tree-woman. "I know. When the Giant came this way, I fell. The earth shook so much. You're the girl who is trying to find him, aren't you?"

"How did you know?"

"Trees know many things. A forest is a city, we talk back and forth. We touch leaves and roots like telephone wires. I'll show you."

With Caroline's help they stagger-waltzed over to a sequoia.

The tree-woman lifted a vine off the bark of the redwood and held it to her ear. "Mmhmm..." she nodded and understood and she let it wrap back in place. "That man you were with is back that way," she lifted her brown arm and pointed. "He's sleeping in the flowers."

"Sleeping?" Caroline couldn't believe it. "Sylas is supposed to be making a Giant movie."

"These woods can affect people," the tree-woman explained. "Anything can happen."

Caroline said, "Should I go back and wake him? How far are we from the Giant?"

The tree-woman laughed. The leaves of her hair swished. She rested her wooden hands on her hips. "You can see him now."

The forest loosened its knit to show Caroline. Like a crowd, all the trees moved their arms to let light fall in beams like cathedral pipes. In the middle, a pine man and birch woman eased aside to reveal a doorway made of sewn branches and twigs. Every plant had a part in growing the tree guarded wall. A red berry holly bush pushed the door open as Caroline neared.

There was a glade inside, mountain birds, tall yellow weeds and a lampshade hill of glittering circus canvas.

"Giant..." Caroline's little voice sounded like a cricket.

Still, he heard, for he began to unroll, his arms outstretched, and he sat up. When he saw her he murmured, "Hello," in a voice that could have been the weather.

She felt like all the air left her body. For that exciting moment she was turned to wax, eyes wide, and the Giant seemed to wear the sky.

*****

"Sylas..." said a feathery voice, "Sylas..."

He woke with a start, "What? Who is it?"

The big dandelions fluttered windmills.

"Sylas..." repeated the voice.

"Who's there?" He stood up, clutching his camera. Something blurred in the corner of his eye, deep in the forest of flowers. "Hello?"

Sylas walked towards it. The air smelled sweet. A glittering appeared in the midst of all the green stems, the lights on a little distant lake. The gold surface rippled the circles of something just submerged.

Stopped next to the lake where there were fall leaves washed ashore, Sylas stared hard at the center. The sun rays came down through the trees and ten foot dandelions.

"I see..." Sylas muttered, "You're hiding from me. You wake me up saying my name over and over again, and now that I'm here, you make me wonder if you're a ghost...It's just an autumn lake."

The glassy lake showed no sign.

"Well, maybe I was hearing things," Silas said. He hoped. It did seem like a game. He forced a smile and turned to leave.

"Sylas," the water called again.

A face made the surface foam and splash. A woman, her long cold metal hair over her shoulders, her neck and her arms emerged. Her skin had the wet shine of a moon pearl. In her hand was a glass globe. "Sylas," she said. "Can you take this to the Giant?"

He strained his eyes.

"When he is in water, throw it to him. You'll know when."

Whoever she was, mermaid or witch or queen of dreams, she blew the thing off her hand and like a soapy bubble, it caught the air, floating to him.

*****

The Giant held Caroline up to the world. He smiled and told her, "I was getting used to talking to myself. Since I've been a Giant it's been hard to hear anyone. But I can understand you perfectly."

She twitched a little spidery leg in his hand. "Does it make you dizzy to be so tall?" she asked.

"No, not at all." He opened his eyes. "I love to see the planet for miles and miles."

She could feel what he meant, but she asked, "But don't you miss the littler things."

"Like what?"

"What I can see, like in the morning the spider webs on the wet grass, or to pick up a leaf to look at it."

He laughed, "Bending bridges look the same as webs and a full tree is just like a leaf to me."

"Oh...I guess it's not so different," she decided, "What you see big is what I see small."

"We see the same," the Giant agreed.

"You could do so much to help. More than circus work. Couldn't you build canals for the city or make towers or lakes or something? Why did you have to leave?"

"Is this why you walked all the way out here to find me? To ask me to go back?"

"Of course not!" she kicked his Giant skin, "I wanted to meet you."

*****

While it washed onto the sand at his feet, it waited for Sylas to get over his fear and reach for it.

In Sylas' mind, visions fitted like cogwheels...A woman living in a lake, huge flowers, the Giant they were all looking for...And finally...he asked himself, "Well, what have I got to lose?"

He took the globe out of the shallows, wrapped his fingers around it and felt its weight. Would it fit in his coat pocket?

*****

"This is the cloud world," the Giant said.

On the end of his finger, Caroline held tightly.

White floaty stairs leaned against his hand.

He said, "You can step off and look around. The clouds will hold you."

She was at such a height. She didn't know if she could believe him. Clinging to the ridges of his fingertip, she asked, "I'm not sure if I should."

"I understand. I know how you learned about clouds in school. They're supposed to be made out of cotton. When you're on the ground they look that way. But the truth is different."

Caroline believed and stretched out towards the cloud.

The Giant said, "I know it seems unreal, but feel them and you can tell. Don't worry. All you have to do is step on."

She carefully put her foot out and leaned herself into it. She found it supported her like a rocking chair. So she left the Giant's hand.

Arms out to balance like bird wings, Caroline walked up the white and gray stairway. After thirty steps, she looked back.

The Giant's shape was scattered with drifts and puzzles of cloud.

"Explore," he said, "Enjoy. I won't be far from you."

She waved, "Okay," as she went further away.

*****

A milk white meadow rolled miles before her. It's just like tall grass, being in the clouds. Little blue and gray birds flew out in front of her as she ran.

She climbed to the top of a hilly bank and looked down. A big clear lake was made where there was a hole in the clouds. The green Earth showed through from below.

This is how the angels feel, she thought. Playing up here and looking down.

Around the edges of lake, Caroline began to notice hazy dots moving in parts of the clouds. She shadowed her eyes with her hand to better stare. It might be a flock of sheep, but how could sheep get up here? The same way as me?

She went slowly down the hill.

It was a long way. The sheep down on earth like to eat flowers so she picked the snowy ones that grew around her. She carried a clutch of them, getting nearer to the cloud-animals. They moved along lazily in the gray shadowed valley.

She sung a movie song as she skipped along a wall of cloud until something moved out from it.

A white sheep popped up only a few feet away and pondered her.

"Hello," Caroline said, "How are you?" To show her friendliness, she offered the flowers.

"How did you get here?" the sheep said lazily, slanting its eyes curiously.

"My friend the Giant lifted me."

The sheep took a bite out of the flowers. "Which one?" he munched.

"There's another? Where's the other one?"

"The man is in the forest, the woman is

living in the desert. She's just as tall as him. They both keep bumping into the clouds. I know a sheep who was bumped a mile by a Giant popping through."

"Where is the desert where she lives?"

"It's not that far," the sheep pointed his hoof, "Just follow the clouds over there."

"I've got to get back to the Giant and tell him. Thank you, sheep."

"Thanks for the flowers," said the sheep. He shuffled off and into the thick white.

As Caroline ran, she called out to the Giant. It was easy to stumble on the shifting cloud field. There were pockets of the world showing below, patterned like a checker board. Caroline jumped off the edge of one cloudy step and she missed the next one.

"Giant!" she yelled. She was falling, tumbling. "Giant!"

In the middle of the kaleidoscope, she could see him. It was okay. He reached out and she landed cupped in his hands.

"You didn't have to worry," he said. "I wasn't far, I knew where you were."

Caroline had to catch her breath and keep her head from flying off.

She was small as a grain in his hold.

"I'm sorry you fell," he told her. "Are you alright?"

She watched the sky popping cameras. At the end of dizziness, when she could speak again, she told him, "I have to take you somewhere."

The Giant started to smile, but caught it. She was standing in his hand like a dandelion seed.

"I can see it from here," she said. The

horizon smudged into a lighter color. "It won't take us long."

"Alright," the Giant smiled at her. "You can ride on my shoulder and tell me the way."

*****

In the rocking yellow top of a flower, Sylas put the camera to his eye.

The Giant filled the lens.

"Amazing..." Sylas held his breath and pressed the trigger to film. It whirred.

The Giant tapped his mountain slope shoulder and slowly began to move away. The trees and flower stalks trembled in his wake.

When he was all gone, Sylas let a few more seconds roll before he stopped the camera. "Beautiful shot," he told himself. He laughed and scratched his hair before he realized, "Hey! He's getting away!"

The flower wobbled with his shifting weight as he tried to stand to climb down it. He bounced like a moon astronaut.

Suddenly the sky was orange and doors whooshed open and closed. A black vine came down and desperate for balance, Sylas held on.

Up he went. The air bellowed kettles.

As the ground fell away, Sylas yelled and looked above. The great orange and black stain-glass wings of a butterfly clapped. Sylas was scuffed along the fir tops, dragged higher into the air.

*****

"So you won't tell me where we're going?" the Giant asked.

"It's a secret," Caroline said. She glanced at the horizon. She took out that picture she found in the river. The woman inside the frame was chalky gray and white. It didn't look like the photograph could say anything.

The Giant guessed, "Are you taking me into the desert, Caroline?"

"It's a surprise!" she said. "It's not fair for you to look ahead. Just look at the ground. I'll tell you when to look up and see where we are."

"Okay..." he said. He looked at the clouds and the wreck of trees as he trudged. Dandelions grew immediately in the footsteps he left.

*****

Below Sylas, the ground blurred green. The butterfly rollercoastered so crazily that Sylas couldn't hold on much longer. He had seen plenty of butterflies flap around gardens, but he never expected to be riding one, about to fall a thousand feet off of one. "Killed by a butterfly!" he gloomed.

But amid the tree and sky whirl, he could see the Giant getting closer. The butterfly seemed to be heading for him. Like a paper fluttering kite being reeled in.

Soon, the butterfly orbited the Giant like a moon. The bright wings fanned close to the Giant's shoulder.

"Look at that butterfly!" Caroline shouted.

The Giant stopped and the forest stopped rumbling. He could see a butterfly with a branch of pollen caught on its leg.

"It's Sylas!" Caroline said.

The butterfly let go.

The Giant watched the little man fall off into the air and he reached his hand out for him.

Sylas landed on his back onto a palm field. He stared up at the clouds in a daze.

"You're the second person I've caught from the sky," the Giant's voice rustled.

"Thanks," Sylas said. He felt like Fay Wray in King Kong's hand. As soon as he could move he checked his camera. It seemed to be okay.

"He wants to make a movie about you," Caroline said.

"Oh..." the Giant sighed, "I don't know about that."

"No, it's okay. Sylas makes good movies," Caroline replied. "He told me about them. They're famous."

"Well..." Sylas swung his camera modestly, "They're famous in an obscure way."

*****

276

Not much time passed and already the trees of the forest had become a thin green line on the horizon behind them. The Giant walked on red dry ground. Both Caroline and Sylas rode in his cupped hand watching the big world.

Sylas let some of it roll into the camera.

"Look..." the Giant spoke, pointing his finger, "Can you two see what I see?"

"It's a truck or something," Sylas noticed. "Off the road."

"I see it," said Caroline.

The Giant took them along the gray seam of one lane tar that crossed the ground. There were coppery juts of rock cropped out of the desert land. Beached close to one was a silver touring bus.

The tires were stuck in the sand. A little crowd of people excited around it.

"They need help getting back on the road," said Caroline.

Sylas leaned over the timber sized thumb to read the red-white-and blue letters painted on the side of the bus. "Barry Mario!" he laughed out loud. "It's Barry Mario's tour bus!"

"Oh no," rumbled the Giant's voice. When he was Sherman Pond, working in the factory, the treacly pop songs of Barry Mario played on the radio. Day after day, gritting his teeth, he'd be forced to listen.

"Barry Mario's stranded in the desert!" Sylas laughed. "It's perfect!" He raised his camera again.

The people around the bus agitated like magnet filings and there in the middle, with the yellow puff of hair, was Barry Mario. His soprano voice bleated pleadingly to the heavens.

Sylas was choking with laughter as he tried

to film. The Giant was wondering what tornado damage his foot could do, when Caroline caught them both by surprise.

"You can pick up the bus and move it back onto the road, can't you?" she asked.

The Giant looked at the miniature girl and was forced to decide. Here was the scene: the bus was scribbled off into the soft dune and rock, the whole wretched band of Barry Mario was ship-wrecked. Surely disaster awaited them. In his mind, the terrible and satisfying fantasy of a flattened tour bus, buzzards, no survivors...All those hours of radio songs played and replayed... What a dilemma...But Caroline knows I can't be a part of anything that's wrong...

"No!" begged Sylas as he felt the Giant begin to bend a helping hand. This was supposed to be a defining scene in the film. "You can't *save* him!"

With his free hand, the Giant easily lifted the bus and set it on the road. He bit his lip to see Barry Mario frolic. He couldn't watch. Oh well, at least he made someone happy.

The Giant turned numbly from the sight so they could resume their journey. Parched six foot dandelions grew and wilted in his footprints.

*****

Caroline's sweater pocket buzzed like insect wings. She was sitting on the hill of the Giant's thumb. Sylas was filming from one of the Giant's fingers. She took out the cause of the sound, the golden frame, and faced the woman inside.

"Do you see a lake?" asked the ghostly woman.

Caroline looked into the heat shimmering sand rolls. The clawed and parched land seemed everywhere. Maybe my eyes can't see far enough, she worried.

She palmed the photograph to ask the Giant, "Can you see a lake anywhere?"

"A lake in the desert?" he said skeptically.

"Like an oasis?" said Sylas. All his camera saw was dry everywhere.

Caroline felt the picture talk to her once more. It said, "When he sees the lake, tell him to go there."

The heavy crunch of the Giant's walking stopped. "I do see a lake," he said. "It's hard to believe, but it's there."

"That's where we need to go," Caroline informed him. "When we get there you'll see." The picture in her hand got very warm for a second before she put it back in her pocket.

*****

The reflection of the Giant fleeced over the water in a cloud that grew as he approached across the beach. He stopped at the edge and his feet sunk in the lake. "This is your mysterious place?"

Caroline looked over his hand and answered, "Yes." The desert had turned into the silvery wide pool of a lake. It was so papery smooth. Not even a bird or ripple crossed the glazy surface.

"What am I looking for?" the Giant asked.

Caroline was searching too.

The purr of Sylas' camera started again.

The Giant was about to say something when his eyes caught on the sight of a swirl.

All three of them gasped as waves poured away from the emerging island of another Giant, a woman.

"Sherman," her familiar everything spoke to him, catching the wind like a factory.

He sat down on the sand, almost forgetting the little man and girl in his hand. By collapsing his arm, Sherman set them next to him. He couldn't say her name. He could barely believe it was her.

Caroline recognized the woman from the picture, the woman who now was larger than a house. Why did the Giants shy and stare at each other and look away? What were they afraid of?

Inside Sylas' coat pocket he felt a digging chirp. He recalled the glass ball he hid in there. It buzzed urgently in the cloth like a honeybee. First though, he put the last roll of film in his camera.

"Go on!" Caroline said, "She's been waiting for you."

The Giant Sherman Pond stood and waded

into the water. To stand next to Ethyll again after so long felt like a dream of time, trying to return them to a place they used to know. Was it happening this way or not? He wasn't sure what thought to listen to.

*****

The sound of the desert was shrill with wind on the way.

Sylas was running the last feet of film. He had just enough time for the end.

In the water, the two Giants stood close. Close enough to hold each other, they were still waiting for something to pull them together. Whatever magic that is…who speaks first, who reaches out? They didn't seem able to communicate, like telegraph poles with the lines cut.

On the shore, a skittery girl danced as she watched them. Far out in the lake they were as towering as castles to her. She reached down and threw a handful of sand their way. It hung in the air like a swarm of bees.

Then something ever so small splashed in the lake. Sylas lowered his arm. It was a good throw. The globe left a circle of waves. He waited with his camera ready. A few seconds peeled. A thick pour of clouds came from the splash. Fog began to fill out like the footage of an atom bomb mushrooming

The Giants disappeared in the potion, everything blanketed away from sight, becoming white and a tumbling, cloudy gray.

The wind had to blow the clouds away and it took as long as a theater curtain opening to reveal the desert again, where the lake and the Giants were gone from the scenery.

THE END

Christmas Day, 1995

The author at the time of writing *Rome Used To Be The World*, 1995. This was in the basement of Mike Paulus' house in Portland, Oregon where we converted a cement space for our Super-8 editing room.

Annabelle Barrett is a studio art major at Western Washington University. She enjoys working with printmaking media and watercolor. When she isn't in the studio she is making a killer butternut squash soup and reading mystery novels.

I CAN ONLY IMAGINE

I Can Only Imagine (1993)
Keep Up Your Spirits (1994)
The Sun Does Shine (1994)
White Russia (1995)
Rome Used To Be the World (1995)

Books by Allen Frost

Ohio Trio (Bottom Dog Press 2001)

Bowl of Water (Bottom Dog Press 2003)

Another Life (Bird Dog Publishing 2007)

Home Recordings (Bird Dog Publishing 2009)

The Mermaid Translation (Bird Dog Publishing 2010)

The Selected Correspondence of Kenneth Patchen edited by Allen Frost (Bottom Dog Press 2012)

The Wonderful Stupid Man (Bird Dog Publishing 2012)

Saint Lemonade (Good Deed Rain 2014)

Playground (Good Deed Rain 2014)

Roosevelt (Good Deed Rain 2015)

5 Novels (Good Deed Rain 2015)

The Sylvan Moore Show (Good Deed Rain 2015)

Town in a Cloud (Good Deed Rain 2015)

A Flutter of Birds Passing Through Heaven: A Tribute To Robert Sund edited by Allen Frost and Paul Piper (Good Deed Rain 2016)

At the Edge of America (Good Deed Rain 2016)

Lake Erie Submarine (Good Deed Rain 2016)

The Book of Ticks (Good Deed Rain 2017)

I Can Only Imagine (Good Deed Rain 2017)

Also published by Good Deed Rain

and Light poetry by Paul Piper (2016)

I hope you have enjoyed these books. There are more on the way.

9 781640 072770